SCRUBS ON SKATES

SCRUBS ON SKATES

Scott Young

An M&S Paperback from
McClelland & Stewart Inc.
The Canadian Publishers

An M&S Paperback from McClelland & Stewart Inc.

Copyright © 1952 Scott Young
Copyright © 1985 Scott Young

Reprinted 1999

All rights reserved. The use of any part of this publication reproduced, transmitted in any form or by any means, electronic, mechanical, photocopying, recording or otherwise, or stored in a retrieval system, without the prior written consent of the publisher – or, in case of photocopying or other reprographic copying, a license from the Canadian Copyright Licensing Agency – is an infringement of the copyright law.

Canadian Cataloguing in Publication Data

Young, Scott, 1918–
Scrubs on skates

ISBN 0-7710-9088-9

I. Title.

PS8547.095S37   1985   jC813'.54   C85-098446-7
PZ7.Y68Sc   1985

We acknowledge the financial support of the Government of Canada through the Book Publishing Industry Development Program for our publishing activities.

Cover design by Pronk & Associates
Cover illustration by Rob MacDougall

Printed and bound in Canada

McClelland & Stewart Inc.
The Canadian Publishers
481 University Avenue
Toronto, Ontario
M5G 2E9

Scrubs on Skates

CHAPTER 1

When Pete heard his father's voice in the hall downstairs he was up from his homework like a shot. He came down the first flight of stairs from his attic room two at a time, a fair-haired, slight, wiry boy with the quick sure movements of an athlete. He walked quickly along the hall carpet past his parents' room and his sister's room, and he could see her head bent over her desk as she worked at homework too so she could go to a movie that night. Then he was on the main stairs, taking them two at a time, too. He was halfway down when he saw his father's face.

"I'm sorry, son," he said. "I got the final word today. We can't do anything about it. They won't let you go back to Daniel Mac."

Pete came down the rest of the stairs slowly. Mother was hanging up Dad's coat and hat. She turned and her dark eyes were full of compassion because she knew what this meant to both of the men in her family. She didn't say anything. This was between them. Pete sat on a hall chair and stared at his father.

Michael Gordon was an adult version of his son, a trim, erect and friendly-looking man. Hard work in a big law practice had etched tired lines around his eyes. Sometimes you couldn't notice those lines because of the man's natural charm, but now you could see the lines, as he paused taking off his overshoes and looked at Pete.

"I did all I could, son," he said quietly. "The Board of Education said they saw our point, and everything, but they just couldn't make an exception in one case or they'd have a dozen more on their necks." He paused, then said reluctantly, "That was our last shot, son. You'll have to keep on at Northwest, I guess."

"Your dad tried hard," Pete's mother was trying to break his silence. "Nobody could have tried harder."

"I know, Mom." Pete said, staring now at his shoes. "Thanks, Dad, anyway."

He got up and went slowly back up the stairs. Sarah, his sister, who had her mother's slim figure and her father's fair hair and complexion, was standing at the top of the stairs, one hand on the banisters. Pete saw by her eyes that she'd heard, but she didn't speak.

Pete went past her and back up the second flight of stairs to the room that had been built for him specially in the attic of this house as soon as he was old enough to have a room of his own. He closed the door and stood a minute looking around at the room. There was so much Daniel Mac in that room that it made his throat feel funny to think that now his last chance was gone to go back to that school. It was one of the twists of fate that when the new Northwest High School had opened this year, their home had fallen just one street within the area it was to serve. And he'd been looking forward so much to this winter at Daniel Mac, talking with his friends about what a cinch it should be to win the provincial high school hockey trophy for the second straight year, talking, hoping, figuring, anticipating. . . .

He sat down at his desk and flicked on his radio, but he scarcely heard the words of the disc jockey or the rock group that followed. Without even looking around at the walls of his room he was thinking of everything there – the pennant from winning the Inter-High track meet last spring, when he'd won the hundred and had been anchor man on the winning relay team; the picture of the hockey team after they beat Brandon in the Manitoba final at Brandon; the picture of him scoring the winning goal in the city championship, against Kelvin, a picture that had been in the paper. His father had gotten a print of it for him. And there were other pennants and crests and pictures that were much older, a generation older, dating from the time his father had been an outstanding athlete for Daniel Mac, too.

There was a tap at his door and his sister came in and sat on another chair. Sarah was a year younger than Pete. This was to have been her first year at Daniel Mac. She was bright and popular, had been looking forward to her first real shot at theatre arts – the Daniel Mac teacher was the best in the city. She'd wailed at the transfer, too. But now she tried to cheer him up.

"Well," she said, "now we know what's what we'll have to make the best of it."

Pete said nothing.

"Are you going to try out for the hockey team now?" she asked.

He said, "I feel sort of queer about it now. When the coach asked me before, I told him about Dad trying to get us back to Daniel Mac. They've had five practices already."

"There's one more before the first game," she said. "Anyway, you don't have to worry. . . . You'll make the team all right."

He half grinned. He knew that. One of the oddities of the new school was that he was the only hockey player with a reputation who had been caught in the transfer. The others were boys who either were in their first year of high school or hadn't been able to make it with the other teams in previous years.

"Heck," she said, "they'll have a welcome mat a mile long out for you. One of the boys is in our room, a defenceman, Vic DeGruchy. He asked me once before why you didn't come out for the team."

"What did you tell him?"

"I told him why."

Pete was silent again.

"In fact," Sarah said, watching her brother, "he said something about it again. He seemed sort of sore that you hadn't turned out for the team, as if you were a traitor or something."

"Go away," Pete said. "Nothing personal. I just don't feel like talking."

She got up, not offended, and came over and stood near him. They had always been good friends, but this change hadn't been as hard for her as it was for him. But he was too mixed up in his own thoughts to pursue the question.

"DeGruchy told Bill Spunska, a new boy who wants to play, that the next practice is tomorrow night," she said. "Why don't you just turn up down there and show them how a real hockey player operates?"

"I guess I will," he said, not brightening a bit. "Darn it all, anyway."

CHAPTER 2

The next afternoon at the rink, an old structure used mainly for practices and minor hockey, Pete stood slightly apart from the other members of Northwest's hockey team, rubbing his skates thoughtfully on the scarred wood of the aisle floor. On the ice a few feet away, in that uniform he knew so well, Daniel McIntyre Collegiate's hockey team, the Maroons, sped through the closing minutes of a practice, a big, confident, well-dressed outfit with the stamp of champion on every player. Pete felt uncomfortable and strange in one of the indecently new uniforms of Northwest High.

The other Northwest players were grouped a little apart from Pete. He felt this, and yet it was natural, because he hadn't turned out for earlier practices and scarcely knew any of the other players. He sat alone and looked around the familiar old rink, the sharp sunshine of Manitoba diluted so much by the high and dirty windows that even with the help of a few electric lights the light was bad. The rink was built in the form of a covered bowl, the three thousand high-backed bench seats fanning out from the boards enclosing the ice.

The buzzer rang. Four o'clock. The Daniel Mac practice was over. The gate swung inward and the heavy thump of skate blades on wood sounded through the rink, the panting, steaming talk of the Maroons as they streamed toward their dressing room through the silent band of Northwest players. Then Ron Maclean, star defenceman on the Daniel Mac team, yelled, "Hey, fellows, here's Pete!"

They clustered around him, most of them taller than his slightly built five feet eight inches. He rubbed a big hockey glove over his fair hair and smiled at them, feeling with a deep pang the comradeship among these boys. They all had something to say to him, because he'd been one of the main reasons for their big victories last year, first in the Winnipeg Inter-High hockey league, and then in the provincial playoff against Brandon.

"Do you ever look funny in that getup!" Ron said, laughing.

"Gosh, Pete, couldn't you work it to get back with us?" asked another.

"What kind of a place is this Northwest, anyway?"

And so on. He couldn't begin to answer all the questions, so he didn't try. "Gotta go, gents," he said. "Gangway!" He was going to say something flip, suggest that they should stick around and watch a good team practice, but he couldn't get the words out of his throat. He hadn't known until now how much that old bunch meant to him.

The Daniel Macs couldn't see what was in his mind, of course. They watched him vault the boards and pick up a puck and speed toward goal, and then, talking and shaking their heads at the sad fate of their old teammate, they disappeared through the passage into the dressing room.

Two men had watched the scene. They had been talking, one sitting on the rail and one leaning over it, when the Daniel Macs stopped and talked to Pete Gordon.

The man on the rail now dropped down to the ice. He was big, with square shoulders and a deep chest. He had red hair and wore hockey skates, old flannel pants, and a faded Toronto Maple Leaf sweater. He watched Pete stickhandle easily in on top of the goalkeeper and slip the puck into the net, and then the boy skated listlessly down the ice.

The man at the rail, small and sandy-haired, was Lee Vincent of the *Telegram*. He said, "You got one break, anyway, Red. Getting Pete Gordon."

"I hope so," Red said.

"Well, gosh, you've got him! He's the best high school centre in Manitoba! What do you mean, you hope so?"

"He doesn't exactly look overjoyed to be out there in a Northwest sweater," Red said. "And he didn't come out for the earlier practices. It's just been made definite that he's got to stay in this school."

Lee was thoughtful. "He's a good kid. He'll snap out of it."

"Oh," Red said, "he'll score a few goals for us, I'm not doubting that. He might even be the difference between losing them all or winning a few, if he tries hard enough." He shook his head and skated to the centre of the ice, tooting briskly on his whistle. What he'd been going to say about any boy who wouldn't turn out for a hockey team right off the bat, when he was good at the game, he kept to himself.

The two goalkeepers, ponderous in their thick pads, lumbered from each end of the rink. The rest of the team gathered around him. He looked at the faces silently; he thought of what he knew about these boys after five practices. They were all untried in competition, except Gordon. Everybody in Manitoba knew Gordon, and most of them figured it was a break that couldn't be bought with money that the new Northwest High School had Pete Gordon's home in its area. Red could only hope the break would turn out to be better than it had seemed so far. His eyes stopped at a big dark boy who was watching him intently, another besides Gordon who hadn't been out to any earlier practices.

"What's your name?" Red asked.

"Bill Spunska, sir."

Red looked at him hard. The boy spoke with an English accent. Spunska's face was square, his hair straight and black, eyes dark, and he was wide in the shoulders and thick through the rest of his body.

"You haven't been out to a practice before, have you?"

"No, sir. I started to Northwest yesterday. My parents just moved."

"Where were you before?"

"River Heights, sir." It was a junior school, near Kelvin.

The other boys, some of them, grinned, probably at the repetition of the word *sir*. They called him "Coach," or "Mr. Turner."

"Play hockey there?"

The boy flushed painfully. "Not much, sir."

Red noted the flush with curiosity, then turned back to the others.

"Now, look, fellows," Red said. "I want to tell you something, this being our last practice before we play a game. I want you to take it without getting discouraged, but it's just as well that we all understand one another before we start. As you all know, this is the first year for Northwest in Inter-High hockey competition. It may be a tough year."

He paused and looked around at the faces, some chewing gum, some not, all intent, one boy scratching his head, another with the tip of his stick on the ice and his chin resting on the other end while his eyes never left Red's. Hopeful, excited eyes, all of them. Boys' eyes.

"You boys can all play hockey, after a fashion," Red said. "Every boy in this country can play hockey if he wants to, start young and play all winter on corner rinks and vacant lots and on the streets. But playing that kind of hockey, and playing hockey for a team, are two different things. I don't think any of you, except Gordon, has ever played organized hockey before. Am I right?"

One of the goalkeepers moved, but said nothing.

"I forgot, Paterson," Red said. "You were with Kelvin last year."

"Just sub goalie," the boy said. "I never got into a game."

"You'll get your chance now to get into games, Paterson," he said. "Now, I want to tell you all something. We're a new school, small.

Our enrolment isn't half what the others in the league are. We might take some pretty bad lickings this year. But if we take those lickings the right way, fighting every inch, every game, we'll eventually have a hockey team that'll win a few." Red looked around again at the sober faces. "I don't think there's a man here lacks guts. But we'll need all the guts you've got before this season is over." His glance paused a minute on Gordon, to see how the boy was taking it, but Pete's face was impassive and unreadable.

Behind that face, Pete was hardly hearing the words. He knew Red Turner had been a great professional player, and probably was a good coach, but he was thinking of Pop Martin, over at Daniel Mac, and the way he coached. There was none of this gathering at centre ice for a sermon. Pop always broke the squad into two teams and scrimmaged hard, and corrected mistakes, and then concentrated on shooting and plays around the net. And there was a lump in Pete's throat when he thought of the high horseplay in some of those practices, the confident clumping to the ice for a game, the lively cheerleaders, the school band, the banquet in the auditorium last year when they'd won the provincial final. Pete thought of all his friends and he looked around now at the faces he scarcely knew. A couple of these boys, Paterson the goalie and the tall guy, Buchanan, were in his room at Northwest, but he hadn't seen anything of them except in classes. All his friends were at Daniel Mac, and since school started this fall, every day after school some had come to his house. In this group he felt on the outside. He'd always been in the heart of things at Daniel Mac.

He picked up the coach's last few words . . . "Okay, now, skate a few circuits to get warmed up and then we'll have a scrimmage and I'll try to get some forward lines and defence combinations sorted out. . . . Go!"

The boys went. Most of them went hard, right from the start. Red watched from centre ice and saw that Pete Gordon was letting the others go past him, and in a minute or two something Red had feared took place. The pace of some other boys slowed down to Pete's pace, until several were skating in a leisurely fashion. Red felt a surge of temper that he tried to control, but when Gordon came past the next time he yelled so they all could hear, "Get moving, there, kids! This isn't dancing school! Get going!"

Pete looked up at him, startled, and moved faster. But he kept his head down.

Red went back and leaned on the boards,

where the sharp experienced eyes of Lee Vincent, the sportswriter, had taken in all that was going on.

"I see what you mean, Red," Lee said. "But you've gotta snap him out of it."

"How?"

Lee said, "Maybe you could talk to him."

Red said, "Maybe. I'll try. But talk generally won't make a boy try – it's got to come from inside of him."

Red watched the twenty boys, the variety of skating styles, listening to the sharp cut of the skates going by him, noticing that like most Canadian boys they all could skate . . . all except one. That one was Spunska, the big dark boy with the English accent. He could hardly stay on his feet.

"Say, Lee," he said, "ever seen that big kid, Spunska, before?"

Lee looked at the boy and suddenly snapped his fingers. "Gosh, you've got him, too. He was at River Heights last year. I saw that kid at every River Heights practice, basketball, track, football, anything that I covered, and he never made a team. . . . I don't know anything about him, except that he tries hard."

Red watched Spunska for a minute or two more. "Just my luck that the kid who tries like that can't even skate," he said.

CHAPTER 3

On the sidelines, Lee Vincent moved up into the seats and watched the scene change on the ice below.

Red Turner split the twenty boys into two squads, tossing white underwear tops to one group to slip on over their sweaters to distinguish them from the others for the scrimmage. Lee noticed that Red put Pete Gordon on a line centring two boys whose names were Buchanan and Bell. There was something ludicrous about the way the three stood together. Pete was much shorter than the others. Bell was slight, with thin fair hair and a hooked nose. Buchanan was tall and dark, but thin, rawboned.

Apart from Gordon, whose ability was known and who therefore had to be noticed, Lee thought that the big dark boy, Spunska, was the most imposing figure on the ice. He was an imposing figure, that is, until he tried to skate, wobbling uncertainly towards the blueline.

Now the selection was complete, six men to a side: a goalie, two defencemen, three forwards. The rest climbed into the player bench to wait their turns. Red called two centres, Pete Gordon and Hurry Berton, a squat dark boy, to centre ice and dropped the puck between their sticks. Then he skated backwards, watching the play, a whistle dangling from his lips. Pete effortlessly snared the puck and passed it to one of the tall wingers, who stick-handled in on the defence. Spunska lunged at him and missed and fell to the ice. . . . Pete skated around Spunska looking for a return pass from his winger, but the tall boy, like most of the players on the ice, had learned all his hockey in the swift surging gang play of the corner rinks, where the aim of all was to get the puck and keep it, and despite five practice sessions stressing team play, this time he forgot. He was checked by the other defenceman. Pete, who had been in the clear in front of the net, set for almost a sure goal if he'd got the pass, shook his head angrily and skated back slowly while the play went away from him.

Lee, watching, let the feel of the place get him, as it always did. He listened to the high yells of players calling for passes, the shrill whistle with which Red interrupted play to give instruction to individual players, the slap of the hockey sticks and the crisp urgency of steel skate blades cutting into the ice. A bout of polio in Lee's teens had left him slightly crippled and unable to play any games, but he knew most sports and loved them well, and hockey was his favourite.

He wondered how many hockey players he had watched skating their hearts out in all the rinks throughout the city, checking, shooting, yelling. He saw in his mind the faces and forms of dozens who had played in Winnipeg minor leagues before going on to college hockey scholarships or sometimes going straight to pros, a few as young as eighteen when they reached the National Hockey League.

Local part-time scouts, nicknamed birddogs, would tip a pro club or a college to come and see anyone who showed high promise. From that first look some kids would be on their way. Not all city high schools had hockey programs, but Lee approved of the scheduling policy of the five that did – holding each season to eight games plus playoffs. This got kids used to working hard on fundamentals in the three-a-week practices, playing once a week except at the Christmas break, and having no excuse not to keep up their grades. Lots of time after that for heavier schedules, the two or three dozen games of a college conference, or the practically full-time seven- or eight-month seasons of the major junior leagues (age limits twenty or under) and pro clubs in the big cities of Canada and the U.S.

A burst of action on the ice disturbed Lee's reverie. Pete, checked, had lost the puck at the blueline. The big defenceman, Spunska, lumbered toward it and got the puck at the end of his stick and charged straight down centre ice pushing it in front of him. He really wasn't skating at all, he was running. The two defencemen at the other blueline came together to meet him but Spunska couldn't turn and didn't pass. Spunska hit them. One rose into the air and hit the ice on his rear end and the other defenceman, knocked to his knees, swept the puck clear and back into the centre zone, while Spunska slid all the way into the goalmouth on one shoulder.

Red Turner, half grinning at the awkwardness of the rush, was into the goalmouth immediately, helping the big boy to his feet, questioning him briefly. Spunska shook his head to signify he wasn't hurt and skated back to his own blueline again and the play went on.

When Red changed players on the ice the sportswriter moved down beside the group that had just come off. Pete again was sitting a little apart, but three or four others had gotten together and it was here that Lee stopped, beside a big reddish-haired boy. He'd been playing on defence with Spunska, who had been left on the ice.

"What's your name, son?" he asked.

The boy looked at him, surprised, and then looked again.

"You're Lee Vincent, aren't you?"

Lee nodded. "How'd you know?"

"The picture at the top of your column. I read it all the time." The boy paused, then said self-consciously: "My name is Vic DeGruchy."

"Known as Grouchy DeGruchy," the boy next to him said, grinning.

Lee picked up the first names of the wingers who'd been playing on the line with Gordon, Stretch Buchanan and Henry Bell. Lee stayed with them while they watched the play on the ice, yelling at their friends there, and in a few minutes an intimacy had been built up that was a specialty of Lee's. Boys always were quick to recognize his real interest in them, and that made them talk freely. It wasn't long before DeGruchy said, "I wonder what the heck's the matter with that guy Gordon?"

"What do you mean?" Lee asked.

"He didn't even come out before. . . . Now he acts as if this was something he had to do, like staying in after school or something."

"Maybe it's just because he hasn't got to know you fellows very well yet," Lee said.

"Naw," DeGruchy said. "It's because he

thinks we're a bunch of scrubs. He'd rather be playing with Daniel Mac. . . . If that's the way he feels he shouldn't be out here at all." There was a depth of passion in the boy's voice that Lee felt strongly.

"You shouldn't let it bother you," Lee said. "He'll come around. And when he does, he'll be a lot of use to you."

"A guy shouldn't have to be coaxed to get on a team like this," DeGruchy said. "Gosh, the rest of us were excited when we heard that we'd get a chance with Northwest. . . . I was going to go to Daniel Mac myself, you know. I'd never have got a chance on the hockey team there. Wasn't good enough. But I'll make some of those guys remember me before the season's over."

"That's the spirit, kid," Lee said.

The other boys had been listening, but they weren't as outspoken as DeGruchy. They were still hot from the effort of their time on the ice, and small clouds of steam were rising into the cold air.

"Think there's much of a chance for us, mister?" one of them asked awkwardly. He was a Chinese boy; Lee had got his name, Benny Wong.

"All depends on how hard you try," Lee said. "You listen to what the coach tells you, practise hard."

From the ice, Red Turner called for substitutions and these boys jumped eagerly into the play. Lee got the rest of the names, as the others came off. Then he retired again to his seat a few rows back and glanced at his notes. Lee loved lineups, because to him lineups always told the true story of sport. He read these names now – there were a few he still didn't have, but there were Paul Brabant and Junior Paterson in goal. The defence names he had were Bill Spunska, Adam Lawrence, Gordon Jamieson, Grouchy DeGruchy and Rosario Duplessis. The forwards were Pete Gordon, Stretch Buchanan, Henry Bell, Alec Mitchell, Hurry Berton, Horatio Big Canoe (there was one for you, the tall lanky Indian boy who stick-handled as if the puck was taped to the end of his stick), Pincher Martin, Winston Kryschuk, Benny Wong. He didn't know how many races there were represented there, but now they were all on one team, all trying, except maybe Gordon, and forever after this season these boys like Wong and Kryschuk and Big Canoe and Martin would remember the names on this team and know that people of all races could get along when they had something in common, a puck or a ball.

On the ice, Pete Gordon again was loafing back up the ice from a try on goal, and Red Turner let him have it.

"Gordon!" he said. "Get moving!"

Just that. No more. The others on the ice looked sharply at the coach and moved harder themselves, and Pete, after a quick look at the coach, dug in after the play which had got away from him. In an almost insolent gesture, he caught the puck carrier, hooked the puck away from him, and sped back up the ice. Spunska was one of the defencemen. Gordon shifted to the right and Spunska tied his legs in knots trying to get at him. Gordon outskated the other defenceman, DeGruchy, and cut in hard on the goal. He faked a shot and Paterson moved and Gordon deftly slipped the puck into the open net.

It was a beautiful play. There was a scattered cheer from the other players on Gordon's side. Without looking at the coach Gordon went back to centre.

The coach's yell had cut him like a knife. He'd always been the fastest man on the Daniel Mac team, and when he loafed a little in practice he got away with it, because the coach knew that in a game he never loafed. But this coach didn't know.

"I'll show him," Pete muttered. "I'll show him what these bums are like."

He was surprised at the way he felt. It was something new to him, feeling that he didn't fit in. From the face-off he snared the puck again and went back up the ice and this time he shifted DeGruchy out of position, and the goal was even easier, because Spunska couldn't move fast enough to hamper him at all. DeGruchy fell trying to get back after he'd made his bad move, and when the puck was in the net both defencemen, DeGruchy and Spunska, were kneeling on the ice, pushing themselves upright, and then DeGruchy yelled to the wingers who were opposing Gordon's line.

They were Alec Mitchell, a chunky little player with a fat face, and Horatio Big Canoe, the big Indian. The coach was tooting his whistle impatiently from centre ice but DeGruchy spoke fast to the wingers.

"He's trying to show us up," he said. "He won't pass, because he's trying to make us look like chumps. You both get back fast and drive him into centre. Don't give him room to shift around me. . . . I'll powder him. . . ." He said nothing to Spunska, who had come in on the tail end of the conversation, and then the wingers skated back into position. Both the coach and Pete Gordon had watched this and knew that the conversation had something to do with Gordon. Pete's face was set. They could line up across the blueline five deep if they wanted and he'd score through them every time. . . .

The puck was dropped. Pete again got it from the other centre, Hurry Berton. He drove in on the defence. But Big Canoe and Mitchell were crowding him from the sides, driving him straight at DeGruchy. Gordon could see his wings in the clear, but all the disappointment of these last few weeks was in him now and he was going to do it all by himself. He didn't pass. With a quick change of pace he left the two checkers behind and at the defence he doubleshifted. DeGruchy waited for the first shift but was fooled by the second, and his shoulder barely touched Gordon as he went by.

But everybody had reckoned without Spunska. The big dark boy had been a few feet behind DeGruchy, and nobody ever knew whether he planned it that way or whether it was accidental. But when Gordon was still slightly off balance from the glancing blow DeGruchy had dealt him, Spunska hit him. It was a clean check. Spunska's stick was on the ice, his arms spread wide almost as if he was going to embrace Gordon. He was slightly crouched. He hit Gordon with a powerful forward thrust and twist of his shoulders and chest and the little centreman's skates left the ice and he went down with a sickening thud.

The whistle blew immediately, while DeGruchy was picking up the puck and racing for the other goal. Gordon was writhing on the ice and Spunska knelt down beside him. Red Turner, skating up fast, saw that satisfaction at the success of his check was mixed with apprehension in the big boy's face. Turner grabbed Gordon's legs and worked them back and forth and in a minute Gordon said, "I'm okay," and tried to spring to his feet. But there was no spring left in him. He rolled over and pushed himself to his knees and then stood up shakily.

"You okay?" the coach asked, holding his arm.

"Just winded," Gordon said.

"I'm sorry if I hurt you," Spunska said anxiously.

DeGruchy said nothing. He stood with the puck at the end of his stick and his big Dutch face was as easy to read as a page of big print – he was pleased.

The coach changed players again, sending the others to the sidelines to rest, and then he leaned on the boards watching the play and seeing again that ferocious check. And he was scarcely thinking of Gordon at all. He was thinking that if big Spunska learned to skate (surely not this season, but sometime) just enough to hand out checks like that with reasonable regularity, he'd slow up an awful pile of fast men.

CHAPTER 4

It was morning, two days later. While one of his assistants was taking a class in physical training on the big gym floor down the hall from the sports office, Red Turner was at his desk. One of the student managers, Fat Abramson, had this period off from his studies and was labouring over his equipment records. Abramson knew the scoring statistics of the National Hockey League for as long back as he'd been able to read. No more enthusiastic hockey fan existed in Canada. But he was too light for the game. He weighed only a few pounds over a hundred, with legs and arms like pipe cleaners.

Now the coach looked up and saw Abramson standing in front of his desk.

"What's up, Fat?" Red asked.

"It's that Pete Gordon, Coach," Fat blurted. "He doesn't deserve to be on our team, I think!"

"He's a real good hockey player, Fat," Red said mildly.

"He doesn't want to play for us! Darn it,

anybody who doesn't wanta play shouldn't be on the team!"

Red looked at the intense light in Abramson's dark eyes. There was a lot of passion in this boy and Red knew it. And he was the best student manager Red could have found. The hockey equipment was always fully dried, even if Fat had to carry it all down to the furnace room and back every day himself. After the last practice, two days ago, the day that Spunska hit Gordon that terrific check, Fat had taken the team's long underwear home and brought it back clean. Red had found out the boy had done it himself in his mother's washer and dryer.

"Just between you and me, Fat," Red said, "I've been thinking of having a talk with Gordon. I want you to keep this to yourself, because I don't want to seem to be singling him out for any special attention. I agree with you that he should try harder than he did the other night, but you've got to remember that what he had at Daniel Mac can't just be dropped overboard in a few days. He'll come around, all right."

"He'd better!" Fat said.

Red was curious. None of the other boys had said anything to him about Gordon, but he guessed that what Fat felt would be a pretty sure indication of how the others felt. He tried to lead the boy on a little. "I think the others like him out there," he said. "I mean, he's good, he'll score goals for us."

Fat shook his head vigorously. "That doesn't count! The other guys would rather not have him there at all if he isn't going to try. I mean, they do their best and Gordon doesn't; that's enough to make anybody mad."

Red understood. He'd seen this situation a few times before in sports – boys or men who have to try every inch of the way always half resent someone who can be good without even trying, and doesn't try. It was sort of belittling the efforts of others when someone with all the natural talent in the world, talent the others would trade anything for, treated his talent as if it were nothing to get unduly excited about.

"I'm going to have a talk with him," Red said again. "I think you'll see a change pretty soon. But don't say anything to the others about it."

"I won't," Fat said. "But, sir, I'm darn mad! If he's going to be a good hockey player he's got to get used to things like that. I mean Brad Park played just as hard for Detroit as he did for Boston. And when you were traded from Detroit to Toronto, you didn't quit trying or anything like that, yourself!"

Red grinned. "This is a little different." But he sat back and remembered that time nearly fifteen years ago when he'd been traded, and the original disappointment at leaving the old gang. It had taken weeks before he felt at home with his new club, even though he'd never been treated any better anywhere.

"Not so different," Fat grumbled, and turned back to his work.

In a few minutes Fat left the office, and Red thought about Gordon and what he could say to the boy. He believed that if he put it right up to Gordon, the boy would see it his way and would make the effort. Red went over in his mind what he would have to say. It would be sort of an appeal to Gordon's pride. He'd have to show him how much the others on the team were trying, and how much the team as a whole depended on the efforts of the one really outstanding hockey player.

"I'll talk to him at noon," he said to himself, and pulled a class schedule toward him. Let's see, Gordon was in Room 22, Grade Eleven. They were in chemistry now and would go to French after this period. Red got up restlessly and glanced at the sports pages open before him. Northwest's first game was tomorrow night. The opposition was Kelvin. In a way, Red wished that the first game was against Daniel Mac, because he had an idea that Gordon would want to show well against his old mates. One outstanding game might eliminate the tension there seemed to be now between Gordon and others on the team.

Red left his office and looked in at the equipment room. The football season was over and the uniforms had been cleaned and were packed in trunks. Two dozen hockey uniforms hung now on specially designed hangers – actually just pieces of wood attached to a long rail, with five hooks hanging down below each piece of wood so that each piece of equipment could be hung separately to dry. The sports department was almost deserted now. At noon and after school it was always buzzing with student managers, all of them wrapped up heart and soul in this extra, unpaid work that made them part of the school teams.

Along the hall from the equipment room, the dressing rooms – new as they were – already had the sweaty smell of equipment and liniment. The shower rooms were deserted but in a few minutes would be thronged with the boys who were taking gym classes now. They'd be showering, toweling themselves, changing back into their clothes for their next bout with learning. Red glanced into the gym and watched his assistant, tall, young Tuffy Bowers, putting half a class through work on the horse and mats while the other half batted a volleyball back and forth. The gym also served as the school auditorium, with a stage at one end. In a year or two the stage would be moved out and a real auditorium built, he hoped. Now things were rather complicated, as they must be in a new school. Sometimes at night here Tuffy's basketball teams would be practising on the floor and the dramatic society would be rehearsing on the stage, and the two didn't fit together very well. Especially last night, when a basketball dropped on stage in the middle of Hamlet's soliloquy.

Red looked at his watch again. Tuffy had blown a whistle. That meant five minutes before the period ended. The youngsters streamed off the floor into the showers. Red walked along the wide, modernistically panelled halls towards the chemistry lab. He waited at a spot he knew Gordon's class would pass. He wanted this to look fairly casual, if anyone noticed it.

The high startling sound of the buzzer interrupted work. Classes rushed into the halls en route to other rooms. Pete was near the head of the line that left the lab. He was thinking about the check Spunska had given him two nights ago. In fact, whenever he moved, it was hard not to think about it. He had a stiffness at one side of his neck and a painfully bruised chest where Spunska had hit him. The other boys in the line were talking among themselves.

In the hall, Pete looked at the panelling, the tall blank doors, the fluorescent lights in the ceiling and he was lonesome for the age-old smells he'd known at Daniel Mac. There was something too new about this place. He remembered the kind of reverence with which he used to wander in the halls at Daniel Mac, when he first went there. The halls were decorated, all three floors at the old school, with pennants and pictures. Hockey champions, football champions, champions of the Inter-High track meet, basketball champs, volleyball, tennis, even debating. Daniel Mac had won every school championship in the city at one time or another, and the record was all there for the new students to look at. And the names were there, too, in the halls, great names of old Daniel Mac teams of the past, and Pete remembered how sometimes he'd get talking with his dad, who'd been one of them, and hear about those great men as boys, about their feats of courage and skill on the playing field and the hockey rink.

Turning to go down a wide, shallow, comfortable set of marble slab stairs, lit perfectly by a skylight above, Pet's lonesomeness increased. There's been nobody here before them except the architects and the workmen.

"Pete! Just a minute!"

Pete looked around and saw Coach Turner coming toward him along the hall.

"Yes?" he asked.

"Do you stay at school for lunch?"

"Yes."

"Would you come down to the sports office for a few minutes when you're finished?"

"Okay."

Pete turned away and caught up to his single-file line, falling in at the end. He guessed what was coming. Involuntarily within himself he erected a sort of wall against being affected too much by what the coach would say. He didn't know why he was uneasy, but he was, and he put it all down to the general feeling of listlessness that had come on him with this new school. A lot had gone out of his life. His boyhood had been spent building toward Daniel Mac and then university. Now those hopes had been interrupted and he seemed to have nothing to put in their place.

Just as he was turning into the room where he'd take his French, he caught some words, faintly, as another class of boys passed by. The words he caught were, "Boy, you should have seen the check Spunska caught him. . . ."

He glanced around quickly to see who had spoken. It was that big guy, DeGruchy. Pete's sister, Sarah, was well back in the line, talking with Spunska. Pete turned back quickly and entered the room, and to his general uneasiness now was added some resentment. Why, they were sort of gloating in the fact that he'd been hit hard! He remembered Spunska apologizing after he'd done it. He didn't blame the new boy at all, because it had been a clean check. But he remembered then that DeGruchy had called in the wings before the face-off. That was it – he'd been telling them to run him into the defence. He remembered now that his wings had been in the clear. He glossed over the fact that he should have passed to one of them, but hadn't. He sat down in his seat and opened his French book and still he fumed. When the teacher asked him to read he had to ask the place, and the snicker that ran through the room made him even more resentful. Why, these guys seemed to like seeing him embarrassed.

He silenced them by reading perfectly. He was a good student as well as a good athlete.

"That was very good, Peter," the French teacher said when he sat down.

Pete kept his head down. Even praise didn't seem to help much the way he felt now.

At noon he had soup, a sandwich, pie, and a glass of milk. The clatter of the cafeteria, new and spotless, seemed somehow louder and less homey than the battered old tables at Daniel Mac. He finished his pie and walked down to the sports office.

He had to admit that in equipment, anyway, this place had Daniel Mac beaten. Sports seemed to be almost an afterthought in most of the old schools, but in this one about half of the ground floor was given over to athletics. He tapped on the door of the sports office and the skinny boy lounging inside looked up and Pete was astonished at the look of hostility on his face.

"The coach just went along the hall," Fat said.

"I'll find him," Pete said.

He glanced through the open door into the equipment room, but the only person there was a boy blowing up a basketball with an automatic pump attached to a table. Another door led to showers and dressing rooms, and the coach wasn't in either. The gym was empty. On the way back along the hall he heard voices through a door which said on it, STUDENT ATHLETIC ASSOCIATION. He glanced in. One boy was pounding a typewriter, three others were folding photocopied sheets of paper, and still another was running the big photocopier. The coach was reading one of the sheets and looked up when Pete stuck his head in.

"Right with you," he said. Pete closed the door and waited outside. In a minute the coach came up. They stood there in the hall. Red got right to the heart of the matter.

"Pete," he said, "you can make or break this hockey team. I'm putting it right up to you."

Pete said nothing, looking at the coach quickly with surprise in his eyes, and then looking down at the floor. His thoughts were confused. He tried to sort them out.

"What are you thinking?" Red asked.

"Well," Pete fumbled. "It's just that for years I been thinking all the time about Daniel Mac. I'd do anything for Daniel Mac because, well, it was my school."

"Northwest is your school now."

Pete knew the coach was trying to get down inside of him to see what made him tick, and finally he blurted out, "Well, I guess a lot of it was because of all the friends I had in the school. I mean, they'd be there cheering me every minute. My dad went to Daniel Mac, too, you know. . . . I figured it wasn't fair that I had to switch."

"Your dad tried real hard to swing it so you could go on to Daniel Mac this year."

"I know."

"I want you to know that we didn't do a thing to stop him. It was the school board that ruled you had to go to Northwest because they had to make their rulings stick."

"I know," Pete said.

Red had intended to say a lot more. Now he changed his mind. At the rink he'd told Lee Vincent that talk won't make a boy try – it's got to come from inside him. He knew from looking at Pete that something was happening inside; he could only hope it was what he wanted. "It's up to you," he said finally.

"Okay." Pete turned and walked away.

Several groups of boys were going by and Red watched him merge with them and wondered if the boy could really lose his identity, his old identity, and build a new identity around this bunch of scrubs from Northwest.

When Pete got home after school that night his sister Sarah was in the living room. She had changed to jeans and was stretched out on the couch with her feet up on the back, reading a book. She looked up when Pete came in and when he started up the stairs without speaking she said, "Hey!"

"What?" he asked, from the stairs.

"I've been hearing things about you."

"What?" He came back down the stairs and stood in the living room doorway.

"That you're a sort of a poor type," she said.

He looked at her silently.

"They say that when you finally did go to a hockey practice you didn't even try and that if you'd do your best Northwest wouldn't have a bad hockey team."

Pete tossed his books on a hall table and slumped into a chair and looked at her. "I just can't get as interested as I was at Daniel Mac," he said. "Who was telling you? I suppose it was that DeGruchy."

She laughed. "He's not a bad guy." Then she got serious. "You know, he's the one who's sorest at you, though. And if he plays hockey anything like as hard as he tries in class, I guess it would gripe him if he thought somebody else wasn't trying." She paused. "There's another boy in my room who's been out for the team."

"Who?"

"Bill Spunska."

He grinned wryly. "He's the one who flattened me in the practice the other night. I've never been hit like that in my life before."

"Was it . . ." she began, fumbling. "I mean, it wasn't . . ."

"It was a clean check," he reassured her.

"Some of the other girls say this is only the second year he's ever been on skates," she said.

"It looks like it," Pete said. "I don't think he'll make the team . . . even *that* team."

"You shouldn't talk like that about our team." She got up and moved over to the record player and started shuffling through some albums. "It *is* our team, you know."

"I know," he said. He told her about the coach talking to him, and told her she wasn't to say anything about it to anyone.

They were still talking when Ron Maclean came in about five o'clock. He knocked on the veranda window and raised his eyebrows and they nodded so he let himself in. He was a big red-headed boy who played defence for Daniel Mac, the one who'd stopped to talk to Pete at the practice two days ago. He lived two streets away, just over the boundary between the two schools, and he'd been one of Pete's best friends for years, although sometimes lately Pete hadn't been sure whether Ron would come quite so often if it wasn't for the coincidence that Sarah was usually around, too.

"Hi, junior," Ron said to Pete. "You going to get murdered by Kelvin tomorrow night?"

Pete looked at Sarah and then at Ron. "Don't know," he said.

"You'll get murdered," Ron said confidently. "I looked at that outfit you've got. Not a guy I ever saw before, except you."

"Don't be so sure," Sarah said.

Pete said nothing. But he looked at Sarah and could see she wasn't bantering.

"Look who's the hockey expert," Ron scoffed.

Sarah abruptly left the room. Ron looked after her puzzled, and then turned back to Pete. Ron was sometimes a little lofty when he talked about the Daniel Mac hockey team. He didn't mean to be lofty, but Ron was a great team player, never played for a team he didn't think could lick anybody in the world. For the first time, this afternoon, his ebullient confident talk aroused a terse reserve in Pete. Ron sensed it, after a while.

"Not feeling right?" he asked.

"Not so good," Pete said.

"I don't blame you," Ron said, "playing for that outfit."

He read a magazine for a while, but eventually got tired of laughing uproariously at cartoons, showing them to Pete and getting no reaction. Finally he got up, and with one final reluctant look at the stairs where Sarah had disappeared, said, "Well, gotta get out of this morgue."

Pete didn't get up. Ron was like one of the family. He didn't need attention getting in and out. On the way past Ron dropped a hand to Pete's shoulder and with exaggerated concern said, "Hey, boy, it's not right now you die. . . . It's tomorrow! Not until tomorrow, against Kelvin. Buck up, now!"

Pete managed a wan grin. Then Ron was gone.

Sarah came back down, just as their mother came in the front door. "Some parcels in the car, dear," Mrs. Gordon said to Pete. "Would you mind getting them?"

"Want me to drive down and get Dad?" Sarah asked.

Mrs. Gordon looked at Pete doubtfully. Getting up to go for the parcels, Pete thought, everybody looks at me and if I've died or something. And I can't do anything about it.

"All right, dear," Mrs. Gordon said to Sarah. "You go. It's time, I guess."

That evening was a quiet one around the Gordon home. Pete went up to his room early, mumbling something about homework, followed by Sarah, to her room. Their father watched them go.

"Darn it," he said for the hundredth time in the last ten weeks. "I wish I could get them both back to Daniel Mac."

Mrs. Gordon could only manage a sympathetic murmur she had perfected for replies to this statement.

In his room above the others Pete finished his homework and listened to his radio and then went to bed. He was reading *Moby Dick*, but a book about a shipload of men chasing a whale didn't seem to be what he needed tonight. He put out his light about ten-thirty, and a few minutes later heard his mother come to the foot of the attic stairs and hesitate and then leave, when she saw his light was out.

He was thinking about what the coach had said to him. It was all true, and it was all logical enough. But try as he did, he couldn't seem to make Red Turner's words count for as much in his mind as the long string of hopes and friendships that had been bound up in Daniel Mac. He thought of the game with Kelvin tomorrow night almost with dread, because he recognized that he didn't have in him the taut excitement that he'd always felt in the past before a game.

His last thought before he went to sleep was a hazy one, that he wished somehow he could get that feeling back.

CHAPTER 5

There weren't many people in Winnipeg who were unaware of the celebration on high school hockey nights at the city's biggest rink, the Arena. The cars full of parents and old grads and students flowed in steady streams from all over the metropolitan area, and special buses filed through the streets from each school, every window open to emit the heads of two or three yelling students. At the downtown corner of Portage and The Mall a bus from Northwest passed a bus from St. John's Tech and the school yells and boos and cheers and catcalls rolled down the wide avenue, and window-shoppers and showgoers walking in the light mild snow stopped and looked back and smiled to themselves and at strangers, remembering when they rode in buses to games where they yelled themselves hoarse for strong, trying boys whose names and faces now came back to them from the happy school-day past.

Near the rink, the Kelvin Technical High School contingent rolled in from the southwest section of the city and before the string of buses came in sight the yells could be heard, every voice outshouting another until it was a triumphant roll of sound.

> *Kay Tee Aitch Ess!*
> *Kay Tee Aitch Ess!*
> *Are we in it? Well I guess!*
> *Race 'em! Chase 'em! Eat 'em up raw!*
> *Kelvin! Kelvin! Rah! Rah! Rah!*

The Northwest buses had arrived first and now a hundred or more boys and girls gathered in a heads-down huddle in the middle of the parking lot and gave their yell, the yell of the new school, some fumbling because they hardly knew the words yet.

> *Rackety Rax Co-ax Co-ax*
> *Chuckah Challunx Challunx Challax*
> *Hullah Belloo Bellum Bellah*
> *Northwest! Northwest! Rah! Rah! Rah!*

A young cop directing traffic blew a whistle and came forward good-humouredly and the Northwesters scattered and piled into the entrances to the rink. Buses from Daniel McIntyre and St. John's Tech and Gordon Bell Collegiate unloaded at the entrances, too. You could hear the rumbling noise from inside the rink.

One of the men shoving through the crowd at the door, head tucked into his overcoat, was

Lee Vincent, the sportswriter from the *Telegram*. The doorman waved him in with a word of greeting and he brushed through the throngs. Funny thing, he thought; all the girls look pretty, and all the boys look handsome. There must be something about being young that does that to people. . . . The scuffle of heavy boots and overshoes filled the lobby as he made his way through the jam of parkas, down coats, colourful woollen scarves, ear muffs, and bright expectant eyes. Suddenly he was out of the crowd, heading to the dressing rooms. The Daniel Mac and St. John's teams, who would meet in the second game of the double bill, weren't in the dressing rooms yet. They'd watch the first two periods of the Kelvin-Northwest game and then come down to dress. Lee glanced at the closed doors of the Kelvin and Northwest dressing rooms, hearing the mumble of voices from both, and then he opened the door to the officials' room and walked in.

The referee, Dick Dunsford, looked up and grinned as he came in. "Hiya, Lee." The two linesmen greeted him as well.

"Hello, blind men," Lee said.

The officials were dressed alike, in dark trousers, white sweaters, white shirts, dark ties. Dunsford, dark and wiry, had been one of the best hockey players the district ever had produced and now he'd been refereeing for fifteen years. The others also had played, but not as well.

Dunsford looked at his watch and then all three leaned over and tightened their skates. They stood up, bantering with the sportswriter, and clumped out into the wide corridor. Dunsford blew a short blast on his whistle and the four men, three on skates and one in heavy overshoes, walked along toward the entrance leading to the ice.

Roars and boos greeted the officials. Lee, slip-slipping across the ice on his way to the press box, grinned to himself. He enjoyed a good professional game, but the feeling of these kids always got him hardest. A couple of times in his life, when he had been offered advancement on his own paper or more money from another paper, the thought of leaving junior and high school sports had been the one obstacle he couldn't overcome. At the timekeeper's bench he greeted Arthur Mutchison, the timekeeper, and took the official lineups list that Mutchison handed to him. Mutchison was nearly seventy years old. He'd come to Canada forty years before, the penniless youngest son of a titled English family, and he was a fixture in local amateur hockey.

From lists which the coaches had given to the timekeeper, Lee wrote down the lineups:

NORTHWEST

Starters	Alternates	
Goal		
Junior Paterson	Paul Brabant	
Defence		
Vic DeGruchy	Rosario Duplessis	
Gordon Jamieson	Adam Lawrence	
Centres		
Peter Gordon	Hurry Berton	Pincher Martin
Wings		
Stretch Buchanan	Alec Mitchell	Winston Kryschuk
Henry Bell	Horatio Big Canoe	Benny Wong

He copied the Kelvin lineup, too, and then glanced back at the list of Northwest players. Spunska naturally wasn't listed. He was sorry for Spunska, because he always hated to see a boy try hard and not succeed, but it was no surprise. The boy just couldn't skate.

Gordon was starting at centre. Lee wondered how successful Red Turner had been in stirring this boy out of his indifference. Scanning the lineups, he leaned over to Mutchison and said, "This Junior Paterson in goal. . . . He was Kelvin's sub goalie for two years. Sure be nice if he could win this one."

"Not a great chawnce, from what I am told," Mutchison said in his deep rumbling English accent.

"In any contest between human beings, everybody has a chance," Lee said. "That's my

53

speech for the night." Then he headed up to his seat in the press box.

The noise in the rink was a constant, uninterrupted roar. School yells sounded from all quarters. Each school had a section of seats, and the section for the school that wasn't competing tonight, Gordon Bell, wasn't much smaller than the others. Cheerleaders danced in the aisles, the yells sounding in staccato precision.

Pete was lacing his skates as he heard the referee's whistle outside in the corridor to signal that the game would start in five minutes. He'd been among the last here, because his father had trouble finding a place to park, and DeGruchy had said sarcastically, "We can relax now, fellows, he's here," when he came in through the door.

Now the coach stepped to the centre of the floor.

"I can't say anything now that I haven't said before," he said. "Try hard, Do your best. That's all." Then, as they rose, he added, "Just a minute. That's not quite all. I just want to tell you something about that boy, Spunska, who tried out for the team the other night. He's not good enough to make the team yet, because he's only been on skates one year before this. His parents came here from Europe just last year. But he wants so much to be a hockey player that he talked to Johnny Petersen, the manager, and Johnny gave him a key to the old rink so he can come at six o'clock every morning to practise skating for two hours before he goes to school." He paused. "Just thought I'd tell you that," he said. "All right, let's go!"

When the teams came to the ice the noise rose until it was as if the rink had been silent before. Junior Paterson, the goalie for Northwest, was first in line, bulky in his heavy goal pads, but pale. He tossed a puck out in front of him and shot it down the ice and skated after it. The rest of the team followed him, Horatio Big Canoe, Benny Wong, Martin, Kryschuk, Pete Gordon, Buchanan, Bell. . . . Then Kelvin came, their worn cherry and grey contrasting with Northwest's flashy new red and blue. Kelvin's team was no heavier than Northwest's, but like the other three veteran school teams in the league, it was experienced. Lee, looking up and around, noticed that there were fewer adults in the Northwest section than in any of the other sections – no old grads, of course, the men and women who gave tradition to schools by their feats of the past.

The referees were checking the goal nets to make sure there were no holes through which a puck might be driven on hard shots, a thing that didn't often happen, but when it did, precipitated great arguments, with the scoring team insisting the puck had gone in and the defending team insisting it hadn't.

There were no holes.

The goal judges took their seats behind each net and flashed their red lights to make sure these lights would go on as soon as they pressed their buttons after judging that a goal had been scored.

The teams warmed up quickly with shooting practice and then the whistle blew for the opening face-off at centre. The alternates filed off to the player benches and the starting teams took their positions, the forwards strung across centre ice facing each other, the defencemen on the bluelines. The goalies banged their pads with their broad sticks, waiting nervously.

Pete stood at centre ice waiting for the referee to drop the puck. Usually in the minutes before a hockey game he was as tense as a tight wire, his stomach in knots, and now, like last night, he felt none of that. There was nothing except a sort of emptiness. He glanced over the Kelvin team and recognized the stars from last year: Barker, the big angular defenceman, whose bone-crushing checks he remembered; Keenan, the opposing centreman, who was very short between the hips and shoulders and who stood and skated with a peculiar wide set to his legs and therefore seemed extra hard to knock down; Stimers, the handsome winger, with dark wavy hair, one of the hardest shots in the league.

The referee tooted his whistle and simultaneously dropped the puck and skittered backwards out of the way. Pete made a pass at it but Keenan had it and flipped a pass to Stimers. Pete followed Keenan in, stride for stride, guarding against the return pass. DeGruchy lunged at Stimers and missed and then Pete saw that the other Kelvin winger was speeding in on goal, outskating his back-checking wing, and Stimers's pass came flipping across the width of the rink and hit the other winger's stick and stayed there and Pete, watching for the shot, for a second forgot Keenan. The thickset boy changed pace like a flash and was two strides away, taking the passout to centre, and he beat Paterson with a rising shot to the left-hand corner.

The crowd went wild. The Northwest section sat glum and stunned in their seats. The Kelvin team clustered around Keenan as Timer Mutchison on the loudspeaker system announced that the goal had been scored by Keenan with assists from Stimers and Josephson. Pete skated back to centre with his head down for the face-off. His man had scored that goal as easily as if he, Pete Gordon, supposed to be one of the best hockey prospects in the province, had been the rawest rookie. Pete glanced up at the clock. It showed that after only eight seconds of the first period, Kelvin had scored its first goal.

In the Northwest section, Michael Gordon groaned, "What a bunch of bums!"

"It was Pete's man who scored the goal," Sarah said in a low voice.

"I know! I know! But what about Stimers's man? Never touched him. What about the man on that other wing –" he consulted his program – "Josephson? The Northwest kid never touched him either. What could Pete do?"

"He didn't keep close to his man either," Sarah said.

"The boy shouldn't be playing with this team," Michael Gordon said. "That's what the whole trouble is."

Pete's mother kept silent. She had seen her son play brilliant hockey in the past. She knew that last year, for Daniel Mac, he never would have allowed Keenan to get away from him that way.

In the press box Lee Vincent said to the reporter next to him, "Gordon looked bad on that one."

"Sure did."

Standing behind the Northwest players' bench, Red Turner stared glumly out at his team.

Sitting high in the Northwest section, almost

to where a few people stood behind the last row of seats, sat Bill Spunska. His cheap stiff raincoat, the only coat he owned, was turned around his ears. He held a pair of woollen gloves in his hands and twisted them mercilessly but his eyes never left the swift pattern of play below, and his ears scarcely heard the tumultuous noise around him. The man sitting next to him, a stranger, leaned over to Spunska and said, "Boy, you sure dealt me a body check when that Keenan was going in on defence. You should be down there."

"Sorry, sir," Spunska said.

The man didn't know it then, but he was going to take quite a few body checks before this game was over.

The puck dropped again. Gordon got it this time, with the automatic skill of years of practice at this position, but as he drove forward Keenan blocked him out of the play, took the puck, and passed again to Stimers.

This time DeGruchy hit Stimers but the puck slid through into the Northwest zone and Keenan went into the corner after it. Pete sped after him, annoyed because he knew Keenan was outplaying him. He pinned Keenan against the boards, took the puck, and skated up over the Northwest blueline. He saw Barker coming for him, tried to shift, too late, and was knocked to the ice on his back. His timing seemed away off, terrible. He sprang to his feet just in time to see a pass go from Barker to Josephson to Stimers, who skated over the blueline and shot a flip pass forward to Keenan. The stocky Kelvin centreman coolly decoyed a shot at one corner of the goal. Paterson didn't move. He stopped Keenan's shot but the rebound came right out to the Kelvin centre again and he drove it into the other side of the net, with Pete still yards away.

The noise rose again, deafeningly. Two-nothing, Kelvin, and less than two minutes had been played.

Coach Turner tapped Hurry Berton on the shoulder. Berton and his wingers, Mitchell and Big Canoe, vaulted to the ice and Gordon, Buchanan and Bell came off. The defence of DeGruchy and Jamieson stayed on. Pete walked through the gate to the bench and sat down, knowing that his man had scored two goals in less than two minutes, something that never had happened to him before. With both hands gripping his stick, he stared at the floor. Nobody said anything to him but he knew he'd looked just as bad as the others on those plays. Maybe worse. His legs seemed made of lead, but it wasn't his legs that were at fault.

A roar from the crowd roused him. Big Canoe had the puck on right wing and was stick-handling around one player, around another, shaking off a third who tried to bunt him into the boards. At the Kelvin defence Barker came for him. But just before the big Kelvin rearguard hit, the Indian boy passed across to Mitchell and braced himself for Barker's check and there was a great new roar as Barker went down, instead of Big Canoe.

Mitchell sped in on goal and got his shot away, but it was wide, and then Kelvin stormed back up the ice. But Big Canoe checked the puck carrier, the puck slid back to DeGruchy, and the big Dutchman, his frizzy hair flying and a determined look on his heavy flat face, bolted down the middle. Again Barker took the jolt, after DeGruchy had passed, and this time Big Canoe was in for a hard shot on goal. The Kelvin goalie partially stopped it and the puck fell at his feet. Mitchell tore himself loose from an enveloping check and poked at the puck with his stick and it slid across the goal line into the corner of the net.

The Northwest players stood up and shouted with the rest. Gordon stood up last but there was a stirring in him as the players came back to centre ice for the face-off again. High in the stands, the stranger next to Spunska was gingerly rubbing his shoulder where Spunska had pounded him.

Sarah was yelling with the rest of the Northwest students, hugging her mother, and her

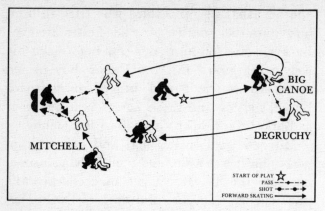

father was smiling a reluctant smile, not knowing what to do in the midst of all this noise. He really wanted Northwest to win and yet there just wasn't the enthusiasm in him. For him, schooled in almost a lifetime of watching Daniel McIntyre teams, it was almost like watching two teams he'd never seen before, in which he had no special interest.

DeGruchy made another spectacular rush, and another. The urge that was in him to win this game stood out as if it was written on his sweater in luminous paint, and that made every time he rushed a sort of violent adventure. But after the second rush Turner knew the boy must be winded and he prodded Rosario Duplessis and Adam Lawrence. DeGruchy came grumbling to the bench, followed by Jamieson.

"Heck, Coach! I was just getting warmed up," DeGruchy said.

He was up on his feet yelling instructions, never sat down until Turner firmly shoved him down and told him to rest. DeGruchy found himself sitting next to Pete Gordon and he turned and said, "You sure looked like a bum on those two goals."

Gordon looked at him in surprise and said nothing.

"We could do a heck of a lot better without you," DeGruchy growled. "If this Berton line had been on then, we'd be one goal up instead of one down, because anybody who was trying wouldn't have let Keenan get in there."

Turner heard the last remark. He was going to tell the boy to shut up but the words died unspoken. Anybody who tried that hard had a legitimate grudge against anyone who didn't.

It was another minute before Pete got back on the ice. He couldn't seem to get going. He wasn't used to Bell and Buchanan and never seemed to know where they were. He heard DeGruchy's words again in his mind and a cold anger possessed him and he hooked the puck away from Keenan and sped in on the Kelvin goal but Barker hooked the puck away and laid a long pass to Keenan at the centre red line. Keenan stick-handled across the blueline and just as Pete got to him he made a long pass to Stimers and the winger got away from Bell and cut in fast around Duplessis. (Spunska gave the stranger in the stands another ferocious body check.) Stimers's low hard shot hit the far post and bounced into the net.

Turner changed lines immediately and when DeGruchy passed Gordon, one coming on, the other going off, he held his fingers to his nose. Pete stopped abruptly and in a split second he considered hitting DeGruchy, having it out right here on the ice, show him he was no coward; and in the same split second he rejected that. This was bad enough. An open fight between two members of one team would be much worse. He skated toward the bench, an angry hard lump in his throat.

Many in the crowd had seen DeGruchy's disgusted gesture. There was a startled long-drawn "Oh-h-h-h!" from those who had seen and a mutter of excitement as they told those who hadn't.

"Oh, gosh!" Sarah moaned.

Her father half rose from his seat, his face red and angry. "What the devil does that boy mean by that? Can't the coach stop that kind of thing? I won't have Pete playing with that kind of a team! I won't! By glory, I won't!" Then the anger faded, and he looked thoughtful.

Pete's mother was silent. She looked straight ahead, watching her son anxiously, trying to see how he had taken it.

Pete sat on the bench shoulder to shoulder

with Bell and Buchanan, both hands on his stick, the tip of it on the worn wooden floor boards, the top of it above his bent head. He heard the excited conversation behind him, not the usual noise of a hockey crowd, and he knew they were talking about him and DeGruchy. Hot thoughts filled his mind. Darn it, that was going too far! All right, he wasn't going so hot tonight! His timing was bad. But they didn't have to play him, did they? They'd been after him to come out and he'd come out, and he was doing as well as he could. But there was a cold thought at the back of his mind that he wasn't doing as well as he could, that no man belonged on the ice when his heart wasn't in it.

A hand dropped lightly on his shoulders. He turned. It was the coach. In that quick sideways glance he also saw Fat Abramson's eyes, the look of disgust and disappointment so strong it was almost hatred. But there was something close to kindness, or at least pity, on the coach's face.

"Take it easy, Pete. You'll get it back. It's just lack of training and practice this year. You can't get your timing all right just in one workout, and one game."

Red didn't change the normal rotation of the lines. For the rest of the game Pete checked Keenan doggedly, his breath coming hard, trying to keep a half-stride ahead of the Kelvin centre, watching him, watching him. Between periods he sat in a corner of the dressing room by himself, talking to no one. The others were silent, too.

Kelvin led 3-1 at the end of the first period, 5-1 at the end of the second, and scored another in the third before DeGruchy picked up the puck behind his own net and bulled his way down centre ice leaving the ice strewn with bodies behind him, and drove a shot at the Kelvin goalie that almost tore the goal stick out of his hands and deflected into the top corner of the goal. So Kelvin won 6-2.

Coming off the ice, Pete was braced for anything. He walked along the lower corridor with his head up, defiantly. He was determined to look everyone in the eye, dare them to say something. But nobody looked at his eyes. Nobody accused him of anything. DeGruchy sat in an opposite corner of the dressing room and talked to a group around him, telling them they'd been going better at the end, they'd be better next time, and Pete noticed that the coach was listening to DeGruchy, too, and that he had an oddly pleased look on his face when he listened. Pete showered and dressed and the only one who said anything to him at all was Spunska, who had managed to get to the dressing room, too, and Spunska said, "That was too bad. But we tried. We'll do better."

"Next game next Friday," the coach called. "St. John's Tech. Let's think about it, be ready for it."

Some of the boys rushed through dressing and got out to mingle with the crowd before it went back in to watch the second game. Pete lingered. When he heard the clumping of the Daniel Mac and St. John's teams going to the ice, and the roar from the crowd, he knew the lobby of the rink would be deserted and only then he left.

His parents and Sarah were waiting. Pete tried to make his voice natural. "Going to wait for the Daniel Mac game?" he asked.

"Don't think so, son," his father said. "Got a big day tomorrow, for me. Early to bed."

Pete's mother put her arm around his shoulders, seeing in her son's eyes at least some of the pain he was feeling. She gave him a good squeeze and then let him go. Sarah took his arm and hung on to it as they left the rink, but she said nothing.

At home, when they were all having cocoa and cookies around the dining room table, Pete's father said suddenly, "Would you rather quit hockey altogether, son? I mean, rather than play for a team you don't really care about?"

Pete was raising his head to answer when Sarah spoke up, almost angrily, "Of course he wouldn't!"

"I'm asking him."

"I don't care!" Sarah said. "That's our school now and Pete wants to play for it. And he'll get used to Buchanan and Bell pretty soon and try just as hard as . . . as . . ." She stopped.

Pete, looking across at her, saw that she had that brightness in her eyes that meant that with one more word, if she couldn't stop herself, she'd bounce out of the room crying. It surprised him to see how strongly she felt.

He excused himself abruptly and went up to bed. There, in his room, where most of his dreams and plans of boyhood and youth had been born and nurtured – and it was plain from the evidence of the trophy-hung walls that many of the dreams had already come true – he thought of DeGruchy; he saw the big Dutchman holding his fingers to his nose, and in his sleep much later that night he twisted and turned as if trying to get away from the memory of that derisive gesture.

CHAPTER 6

The next morning when Pete woke, snow was swirling fiercely around his dormer windows and the wind moaned in the chimney. His room felt like the Arctic. He slammed shut the slot in the storm window and leaped back for the warmth of bed all in one motion, before he was fully awake. Then he wondered exactly how cold it was, and that reminded him that there'd be a weather report on the radio at eight o'clock, just before the sports . . .

Sports!

He looked at his watch. A minute past eight. He leaned over to switch on his radio and only then the thoughts came back to him from last night. What could he do? Something had to be done. . . .

The sports announcer's voice gathered volume quickly in the room, talking about the Canadian football playoff in Toronto today. Pete realized with a shock that for the first time in many years Daniel Mac had played a game and nobody in the family knew the score. He knew that downstairs, where his mother would be preparing breakfast and his father reading, they'd be listening, too. And Sarah, if she was awake, would be listening to her own radio.

Most of the broadcast was on football, and the game that would be played more than a thousand miles away this afternoon. Pete, like every other boy in Canada that day, had his side to cheer for in the national final. Of course his side was the West, even the Saskatchewan club, which had beaten out Winnipeg's Blue Bombers in the Western final. So he listened with interest to the pre-game predictions for the big game and then the announcer said, ". . . and now for the local sports scene."

"The Arena was the scene last night for the opening double-header of the high school hockey season. Four of the five teams in the league were in action. The powerful Kelvin team walloped Northwest 6–2 in the first game. In the second, Daniel McIntyre and St. John's Tech played to a 1–1 tie."

The announcer paused, and when he continued he spoke carefully, as if he said this only after great deliberation.

". . . The big disappointment of the night was Pete Gordon. Remember him for Daniel Mac last year? He was the league's all-star centre, and people said – including me – that he was the best young player we'd seen here in years. Those of you who didn't see him last night couldn't believe how bad he looked. He can still skate like the wind, and stick-handle, and pass. When he wants to. But last night it was clear he didn't want to. I hear that his attitude is the result of disappointment that he was moved from Daniel Mac to Northwest. I hope for the sake of his teammates, who tried so hard, that Gordon drops this prima-donna attitude and from now on plays the game the way we know he can."

In Pete's throat, seeming to press hard behind his eyes, was a disbelieving lump of shock and pain. He swung his legs blindly over the side of his bed and pushed his feet into his slippers and for a few seconds just sat there.

Then the reaction came, a choking anger. He jumped to his feet and his mind pummelled the air with unspoken hot words. He'd quit! He didn't have to take that kind of stuff! They had no right to say that about him, for one bad game out of a lifetime! He'd show them. He could skate rings around any of those guys.

A cool thought from the back of his mind said, But you didn't.

And he sat on the bed again.

The worst thing would be facing the people who had heard it, first the family, then the others. But it was Saturday. If he wanted to, on Saturdays, he often slept in. He could stay here, an hour or two, until the man's words weren't so sharp in his mind, or in theirs. . . . But as soon as he thought that, he stood up. By gosh, he *wasn't* a coward.

He walked quietly downstairs. Sarah's door was open. She was making her bed, her radio playing music from the station which gave the morning sports. She looked up at him, started toward him, but he avoided her eyes. He locked the bathroom door and scrubbed his hands and face, combed his hair, cleaned his teeth.

Darn it! Everybody would have heard it. He could imagine DeGruchy turning to someone in his home, saying, "That's what I told you about. . . . He doesn't even try." He could imagine all of them hearing it, the kids at the new school, and the others, at the old school, his friends. They knew he wasn't like that. They'd be mad. Or would they be mad? Was this just what everyone thought, now? He didn't know.

Sarah came to her doorway as he emerged.

"That was . . . too bad, Pete," she said.

He avoided a direct answer. "Coming down?"

She looked into his face as she passed to precede him downstairs. In the dining room their parents already were seated at breakfast. Mother got up. "Eggs and bacon?" she asked.

"Not for me, thanks," Pete said. "Just toast."

Her protest that he always had a big breakfast, especially on Saturday, faded quickly.

Dad said, "Hear the sports this morning?"

"Yep," Pete said, slipping into his chair.

"Try to ignore it," Dad said.

Pete realized suddenly that nobody was really mad. They were sorry, they made protests on his account, but they weren't mad at all; sad but not mad. He ate his toast, not speaking, thoughtful, and finally he knew that the reason they weren't mad, that he wasn't mad now himself, was that what the man said had been right. There was more to it than what the radio said, there was his side of it, but he hadn't played as well as he could, and that's all there was to it, and his family knew it as well as he did.

He tried to figure out how he felt now. His feeling toward the new school was the same. Nothing. It just didn't affect him one way or another. He felt quick, sharp anger when he thought of DeGruchy.

After breakfast, he decided to shovel the walk and the driveway. When he was up in his room getting dressed his father came upstairs.

"I'm going to the law society meeting," he said, sitting down on Pete's bed. "Mother's coming along to join me at lunchtime."

Pete was putting on a heavy woollen shirt that he sometimes used for skiing; over it went a thick sweater; his parka jacket and hood were downstairs. He waited for his father to say more, but the silence was a long one. "Don't let this get you down," his dad said finally. "They'll forget it."

Pete always found it easy to talk with his dad. He always seemed to understand. "Only if I make them forget it, I guess," he said.

Dad flashed him a look of sharp agreement and interest. "What are you going to do about it?"

Pete shrugged. "I don't know yet." He paused. "Heck, I've got nothing against the school." He thought of DeGruchy and turned to look at the picture-lined walls.

"We're always the heroes in these pictures," he said, waving his arms around. "I guess I've let down the side in more ways than one." Then he found that he couldn't really control himself. It was funny, but he'd get talking and something would suddenly make him feel like bawling. He looked at his dad, sitting on the edge of the bed, watching him curiously.

Now Dad spoke, dryly. "This is something I've seen before," he said. "It's never come quite so close to home, but it's true. That is, an athlete is really a sort of public servant. The public has its own idea of what can be expected from a man, and when he doesn't deliver up to the mark the public feels cheated. That's what's happened here. They don't take into account the way you feel. All they see is that you didn't deliver. That's all. And they're sore about it."

Pete knew it was true. There was a wisdom to it that was almost cynical, but it was clear and sharp enough. He almost asked, then, what should he do? But he didn't ask, because he knew that whatever he did had to come from inside himself. Last night had shown that there was no use just going through the motions, without real conviction. That didn't fool anybody.

His dad got up suddenly. "Well," he said, "I've got to dress and go." He headed quickly for the stairs. "Good luck. See you later."

He clattered downward. In a few seconds Pete followed, put on his parka and mitts downstairs, picked up the snow shovel in the basement, and went outside. From a glance at the driveway he could see that it was drifted heavily, but with luck, and maybe a shove, Dad could get the car out. He shovelled some snow away from the garage doors and got them open, then waved good-bye as his dad backed out the car at full speed, snow flying in all directions, and reached the road without stalling.

In the next hour the wind lessened, but the snow fell faster than ever. By the time Pete had finished the long curving walk the driveway was clogged, the wheelmarks of an hour before - less than an hour - almost obliterated. He worked doggedly. He was glad it was Saturday and he wouldn't have to face the school for another two days. By then, maybe the edge would be off. They would have forgotten, a little . . . maybe. Practice Monday night. That would be bad. For no good reason, then, he remembered the look on Fat Abramson's face, the chance look he had caught, last night. Disappointment, accusation . . .

This wouldn't have happened at Daniel Mac! Gosh, if he'd been out there for the Daniels they probably would have beaten St. John's. Sure they would! And now they'd be tied with Kelvin for first place in the league. And today he would have felt good, and he and the other guys would have sat around somewhere, probably right here in his home, and talked about the game. He didn't notice that he had stepped up the pace of his shovelling so that the snow was flying off the driveway and he was puffing and perspiring freely, until someone called from behind him, "Hey Pete! Take it easy! You look like one of those big snow-blowers. You'll kill yourself!"

Pete turned. It was a man from down the street, a man he scarcely knew, but who – like many others in the city – seemed to know him well, through following sports.

"Yeah," he called. The man went on. Pete was back to earth. But Daniel Mac *hadn't* won, and if they won it would have been none of his doing. He was at Northwest, and Northwest had been beaten badly, and they were blaming a lot of it on him. He stopped and blew his nose and wished that he were five years younger and could go out to the corner rink and work this off, skating, checking, showing anyone who watched that he was Pete Gordon, and he was good.

But he couldn't do it as simply as that. He was in a spot and he was unhappy in it, so he had to get out. But how?

CHAPTER 7

At noon, Pete's mother made sandwiches for lunch, and then left in a taxi to join his dad at the law society luncheon. Sarah went out to do the weekend shopping for her mother, and Pete ate a couple of cheese and onion sandwiches and drank a glass of milk. When the paper dropped on the veranda he got it and turned immediately to the sports pages to read what Lee Vincent had to say about the game. His half-realized dread was quickly allayed. The sportswriter had mentioned him only in passing. "Pete Gordon was below form," he had written, "but that's only natural because, due to an uncertainty as to whether he would play for Daniel Mac or Northwest, he got into only one practice before last night's game. When he hits his stride, Northwest will have a team that won't be a doormat for anybody. Any team that tries as hard as most of the Northwesters did last night is going to win a few."

Pete turned on television to the station that would broadcast the football game, grateful for

Vincent's calm assumption that he would and could hit his stride with Northwest. He was thinking of that when there were heavy steps on the veranda. Through the window he saw Ron Maclean's cold-reddened face grinning while Ron stamped the snow from his overshoes. Pete waved for him to come in. In a way he dreaded this, too. But he walked into the hall while Ron got out of his coat.

"Been out?" Ron asked.

"Did some shovelling."

"I slept all morning. Boy! It's as cold as a referee's heart out there!"

Pete led the way into the living room.

Ron slumped into a big chair. "We should have beaten those guys easy, instead of just a tie. Couldn't seem to get going. They backchecked like crazy. We missed you, too."

"We play them next Friday," Pete said.

"They'll murder you," Ron said confidently. "Hey! I woke up long enough to hear the sports this morning. That was sort of rough on you."

Pete tensed but said nothing.

"How can they expect . . ." Ron began, but he was interrupted by more steps on the veranda. He looked out of the window. "Hey, who's this with Sarah?"

Pete got up and went into the hall and Ron followed. The colour in Sarah's face from the cold made her even prettier than usual. Bill

Spunska was carrying two big paper bags of groceries for her.

"You've met Bill Spunska, Pete," Sarah said. "And Bill, this is Ron Maclean from Daniel Mac. Bill's in my room at school," she explained to Ron. "Was I glad to see him! My hands were freezing, carrying this stuff."

"No wonder, with those skinny little gloves, you dope," Ron said.

Bill looked from one to the other shyly as they bantered back and forth. "I am happy to meet you," he said, shaking hands with Ron. "I saw you play last night. You were very good."

"My gosh, don't talk like that!" Sarah groaned. "He's got a big enough head already."

"I don't get much chance to show it when you're around," Ron said.

Pete took the bags out of Spunska's arms. "Take your coat off and come on in."

When Bill spoke, Pete was struck again by the incongruity between this boy's rugged physique and his stiff politeness. It was so different from the free and easy manner of all other boys he knew. "It is kind of you. . . . If I'm not intruding."

"If you can stand listening to Ron telling you how he could have won the game last night," Sarah said, "you're welcome."

When Pete returned from putting the groceries on the kitchen table, Ron was back in his chair, explaining how he scored the tying goal. "I just saw this hole, see, and I let'er go and . . ."

"You hit it for a change," Sarah interrupted, laughing. She was on the couch. Spunska was on a straight chair, sitting forward on it, his hands clasped between his knees, listening.

"It's hard to be a hero around here," Ron grumbled.

Pete looked at him and for an instant his bitterness returned. "At least the guy on the radio didn't say you were a bum."

Ron, for once, was embarrassed. "That's just what I was saying when Sarah and . . . and . . ."

"Bill," supplied Sarah.

". . . Bill came in," Ron said, looking at Pete, getting worked up. "How can they expect you to play your best with a bunch of stumble-feet like those? I mean, those guys, well, they tried hard enough, but heck, they just weren't in it. You couldn't do it all by yourself! Half those guys played as if they'd never been inside a rink before. My gosh . . ."

"We have some very good players," Spunska said quietly. "Some of them are much better than some of yours."

There was a dead silence, and then Ron said, half laughing, "Now, look, that's silly. . . .

We've got the same team except for Pete that won the provincial last year. Those guys of yours, they may try hard, but . . ."

"I think that in one of the two games we will play against you this year we will beat you," Spunska said.

"Attaboy, Bill!" Sarah said.

"Whose side are you on?" Ron asked, turning to her.

"Northwest's, of course," Sarah said.

"For gosh sake!" Pete said. "Let's not start that again!"

There was a brief silence after his explosion. He was aware of Ron's eyebrows lifted eloquently toward Sarah, then Ron struck on another topic of conversation. He began to question Bill.

"Say," he said. "You sound English."

Bill smiled broadly. "Perhaps you didn't hear my last name," he said. "Spunska. Not, I am afraid, an old English name."

Pete looked up, quickly. He was very sensitive about matters of race. He knew that racial bias was mainly an adult ailment, but sometimes you found it in kids, too. . . . But he saw the wide smile on Spunska's face, and now Ron was laughing out loud.

"Sir Algernon Spunska," he said. "The Duke of Paducah! You're right! There does seem something out of place, there."

"I'm Polish," Bill said. "But I went to England when there was trouble in Poland a few years ago. That's why I sound that way."

"Been over here long?" Ron asked.

"Nosy Maclean," said Sarah.

"I don't mind," Spunska protested quickly. "We have been here fifteen months. For the first year my father worked cutting pulpwood in the North. My mother was a maid in River Heights and I was with her at her work. Now our family is back together." He took a deep breath. "It is very good being together."

Pete couldn't think of anything to say. But Ron was unabashed.

"What's your father do now?" he asked.

"He is instructor of German at the university." Bill smiled. "At home in Warsaw he taught English and French. Here in Canada, where English and French are spoken, he teaches German."

"Holy cow!" Ron said. "That bushwork must have been tough on him. I mean, that kind of a man."

Bill shrugged. "He was a supporter of Solidarity, a friend of Lech Walesa. He has done harder things than chopping down trees."

Pete was watching Bill. This explained a lot of things. What a life Bill had had, compared to the way he and Ron and Sarah had lived!

The football broadcast interrupted them.

During the next two hours in the comfortable room, they ate peanuts, drank Cokes, and watched Saskatchewan beat Toronto in the final. They all felt good over that. Bill had seen Canadian football in two autumns now and he seemed as much a fan as any of them. When the broadcast ended it was twilight, the early twilight of winter. Their discussions of the football game died down finally and Sarah said, "I told Bill on the way home about all the pictures and stuff you've got up in your room."

Pete usually was retiring about showing off his trophies and picture gallery. But this, somehow, was different. "Do you want to see it?" he asked Bill.

"I do."

"I now pronounce you man and wife!" Ron shot in, triumphantly.

They grinned. On their way out of the room, Ron got in his parting shot. "Hey, Bill! You'll notice that everything he did that was good was for Daniel Mac."

Upstairs, Bill looked closely at all the pictures and pennants on the walls, and the trophies on top of Pete's bookcase. He asked questions about each picture, and read the inscriptions on the trophies, and when he was finished he looked at Pete, who was standing beside him. "You must be very proud of being able to win almost as many things as your father. And for the same school. I can see how it must have been hard for you to leave that school."

Pete nodded, turning away.

"That is natural," Bill said.

But when they went downstairs, Pete couldn't get out of his mind the hungry way that Bill had looked at all the tokens of the athletic ability of the Gordons, father and son. He was thinking of what he knew of Spunska's life, the displaced years in England, then the other big move, to Canada; and all at once he realized for the first time, fully, how magnificently lucky he had been to grow up on this continent, in this atmosphere, where the road ahead was never complicated by anything more serious than the change from one school to another.

Sarah and Ron were standing in the hall, and Ron looked up at them as they came down.

"Hey!" he called. "You know what this crazy sister of yours said? She won't come to the movie with me tonight unless I promise not to talk about Daniel Mac. What would I have to talk about?"

"Nothing," Sarah said. "That's the trouble." She was half smiling, but Pete could see she was serious, for all that.

Ron yanked his ski cap down over his ears. "I'm going to get out of this nuthouse," he said. And he left.

"I must go, too," Bill said.

He put on his coat and hat. The coat, really inadequate for this weather, somehow didn't detract from the . . . (What could you call it? Pete thought. Dignity?) . . . dignity that Pete had noticed in him today. Bill smiled shyly at Sarah. "See you at school on Monday," he said. And he shook hands with Pete, who was taken unawares. "See you at the practice, Pete," he said.

When he had gone Pete and Sarah looked at each other.

"Quite a guy," Pete said.

"I think so, too," she said.

"I've noticed that."

She tossed her head at the teasing. "Oh, you . . ." She went into the kitchen, to fix the vegetables for dinner, a job she often did when her mother was out in the afternoon. He walked to the middle of the living room and stopped. He thought of how hard Bill tried to play the game. And here he was. Pete Gordon. He could play it well.

He turned quickly and ran up the stairs to his room. When he got there he stood thinking again, not looking around, not sitting down. He stood tensely, thinking of what his father had said about an athlete being like a public servant; of the life of which Spunska had spoken so coolly, that made his own troubles seem so small. He was excited, trying to grasp what was in his mind, trying to put it into words.

He couldn't. But he knew then that he'd go to the practice. He thought of DeGruchy. But he put the thought away. It wasn't for DeGruchy he'd be doing it. It would be for himself. And Spunska.

But he didn't really put it into words until the next day, after church, when he and his father were walking home over the snowy sidewalks.

"I don't want to talk about it if you don't, Pete. But have you thought any more about what you're going to do about hockey?"

Pete hesitated so long, trying to form the words in his mind, that his father said quickly, "Don't say anything if you don't want to."

"I do," Pete said. "I'm going to play." He went on, fumbling. "It isn't for the school, like it was mostly at Daniel Mac. But I've got to play. Other guys want to play well and can't. . . ." He left that unexplained. "And I'm not going to have people say I'm a quitter. I still can't feel the way I did about it at Daniel, but I'm going to play. To show 'em."

After a pause, his father said, "You mean you're going to play for yourself. . . ." He murmured a line of poetry that Pete knew, but couldn't identify. " 'To thine own self be true.' Is that it?"

They turned in at the house and Pete knocked the snow from his overshoes. "Sort of, I guess," he said.

CHAPTER 8

To Pete's surprise, school wasn't too much of an ordeal, Monday. Walking from class to class along the new halls, carrying his books, listening to the teachers, studying, noticing the rather scared seclusion in which he was left by the others in his class, he thought that maybe he wasn't feeling it all so much because now he knew what he was going to do. He saw De-Gruchy once in the hall, but DeGruchy didn't look his way. Other members of the team, when they saw him, nodded quickly and almost with embarrassment. Pete didn't let it bother him. He'd made up his mind. He'd show them. For Pete Gordon, he'd show them. And for Bill Spunska, he'd show them. And for the accusation in Fat Abramson's eyes, and the confidence in Lee Vincent's column, and the impersonal kindness, perhaps understanding of Coach Turner, he'd show them.

The practice was at six o'clock that night, and the Northwest players gathered at the rink early, coming singly or in twos or threes. Benny

Wong walked from his father's restaurant fifteen blocks away and was three blocks from the rink when he was picked up by Rosario Duplessis, who was in his father's car with Paul Brabant and Hurry Berton.

"'Op in, Benny," Rosario called from the front seat. Benny's face was bright and grateful as he jumped over a snow bank to reach the car.

Near the rink they passed Gordon Jamieson and Adam Lawrence, the two tall fair defencemen, pedalling along on their bicycles, slipping and sliding often on the rutted, icy road.

"Don't hit them, Rosy," Paul said. "Sometimes they're all the support I have."

The others laughed, and yelled boisterously at the two cyclists as Rosy took the car carefully around them.

There were two other cars at the rink, Henry Bell's old Duster, bought from the proceeds of his nightwork in a service station, and Red Turner's sedan. Most of the others came on foot and bike through the late-afternoon gloom. Sarah dropped Pete off on her way to pick up their father at his office, and Pete entered the rink with Stretch Buchanan and Horatio Big Canoe and two or three others. The snow was falling softly through the mild evening outside, but inside the old rink was cold and clammy, and a couple of the kids they called rink rats, who hung around cleaning the ice and doing other odd jobs in return for passes to games, were toasting their mitts on the radiators in the lobby, trying to keep warm.

The St. John's Tech team was practising when the Northwesters walked along the side aisle to centre ice and the entrance to the dressing room passages. They were skating hard in a scrimmage, ignoring the newcomers. Lee Vincent sat high up in the seats watching. He waved and smiled at some of the Northwesters.

In the dressing room Fat opened the big trunk and piled pads and equipment topped by sweaters neatly every couple of feet on the benches along the walls, so that all a player had to do was to identify his sweater number and take that spot.

"Hey, Fat! A good idea!" Rosy called. "This is neat, none of that crowding around the trunk for our stuff. Good for you!"

Fat blushed and the coach grinned at Fat's embarrassment at this open approval. DeGruchy came in and grunted, "Hi," and began to undress. They had lots of time, but there was an eagerness in their undressing, in their shouts to one another.

"I'd like to see that St. John's outfit for a few minutes. We play 'em next, you know."

"Hey, Fat! Some tape over here!"

"Got a lace, Fat? I broke this darn thing."

Alec Mitchell, the chunky little winger, was

turning his shoulder pads this way and that. "Five times I've put these on," he kidded, "and I'm still not sure which is the head hole and which is the arm hole."

"Not that it makes much deeference, Meetch," Rosy called. "You would be as good a hockey player with your arm sticking out the neck, as with your head, as you never look anyway where you are going."

Pincher Martin, a very sharp dresser, spent a good deal of time folding his trousers onto a hanger. They kidded him for that. They kidded Rosy, told him he was a peasouper. Everybody was kidded except Pete Gordon.

Pete dressed between his wingers, Bell and Buchanan. He was getting to know them, Buchanan a lot noiser than Bell, but both of them seemed rather reserved tonight. They kept their eyes away from Pete and said nothing. When he was dressing he looked from one to the other of them, and around the room, and felt the solitude which partly had been thrust upon him, and partly he had brought upon himself. Only once he met a response - when he happened to glance at Spunska, who smiled quickly.

DeGruchy, dressed, was starting for the door, although it was fifteen minutes before their practice time, when the coach called to him, "Wait a minute, Vic."

Red was sitting on a stool lacing his skates, and from this position he said, "We've got to have a captain and a couple of alternates. I could appoint them if you want, but I'd rather you elected them yourselves. Fat here has paper and pencils. It won't take a minute. We'll nominate some men and then you vote on them. The main function of the captain or alternates on the ice is to talk with the referee on any questionable decisions – or decisions that we want to question, anyway." He finished tying his skate and stood up. "Open for nominations," he said. "Should have at least three nominations."

There was a minute of suspended activity, silence, while they took in the situation. Then Big Canoe spoke, "I'll say Hurry Berton." Berton was his centreman.

Fat made a note of that.

"I nominate Grouchy," said Junior Paterson, the goalie.

There was a pause then and Pete had a feeling they were thinking of him, the other side of the coin, the one who would never do.

Buchanan spoke up. "Paterson."

Berton said, "Benny Wong."

"Nobody say me," said Rosy Duplessis. "I would be liable to lose my temper with a referee. That would be bad."

They all laughed. There was another pause,

and the players looked around at each other speculatively, some grinning self-consciously, some – those who'd been nominated – looking down. But no further names were given.

"Wouldn't hurt to have three alternate captains," the coach said, hands on hips, a habit with him. "Then we'd probably have one on the ice no matter who was on the bench. How about we vote for a captain among those four, and let the other three be alternates?"

"Good." "Okay." "Sure."

Fat, his jeans hanging loosely from his skinny flanks as he walked, handed around the ballots and pencils. The boys thought, then wrote. Pete held the pencil a minute, thinking of the four boys who had been nominated. Of them all, he knew grudgingly that Vic DeGruchy would be the best leader. Whatever else he did, he had that power to lift a team. It was partly his strength and partly his weakness, this single-minded overpowering desire to make this team fight all the way. At least, Pete thought, it seems to me a weakness because he's against me. But to the others it's all strength.

Fat was in front of him with his cap, waiting. Pete waited another second. Darned if he'd vote for a guy who had done that to him! The instant he dropped the blank ballot into the cap he felt a twinge of regret that he hadn't faced up to it, and yet he hadn't felt like voting for another against DeGruchy, either.

Fat used the top of the equipment trunk as a counting table, then wrote something on a slip of paper and handed it to the coach.

"The captain is Vic DeGruchy," Red said.

There was a brief round of cheering, laughter, and kidding.

"You'll get a letter C to sew on your sweater, Vic," the coach said. "The others will get the letter A."

DeGruchy got to his feet and raised his eyes. "Thanks, fellows," he said. "All I'd like to say is that from now on let's all pull together. All." Pete knew it was a statement directed at him as surely as if it had been written down and passed to him. DeGruchy would never let him alone.

Pete jumped up. "Let's go," he said, and headed for the door. He reached it at the same time as DeGruchy and opened it to let the other boy out. For an instant their eyes met coolly, then the team erupted into the passage, their skates clumping hard on the rough wooden planking.

Red and Fat stayed behind. When they were all gone, they looked at each other.

"Good choice," Red said.

Fat nodded. He started to tidy up the dressing room a little, straightening pairs of shoes under the bench, and then he picked up the bundle of hockey sticks in the corner.

"Funny thing," Red said. "It's not often there's a mistake in a vote like that. Even after only a few practices and one game they know who is the guy who'll never stop fighting out there."

"Yeah," Fat said.

"Just as a matter of curiosity," Red said, "how did the vote go?"

"Only two weren't for DeGruchy," Fat said. "One would be his own. The other one was blank."

The man and the boy looked at each other, then Red looked at his watch. It was still a few minutes to six, when they were due on the ice. "I got an idea we're going to have quite a season," he said. "Even if we never win a game."

"We'll win some," Fat said.

They went along the passage, Fat carrying the bundle of sticks, Red slapping his pockets to see where he had left his whistle.

Pete was leaning on the sideboards a few feet away from the others. This year he might have been captain at Daniel Mac. There'd been talk of it last spring among some of his friends. He noticed with surprise that his teeth were tightly clenched together, and he relaxed them.

A whistle blew on the ice. The St. John's

players streamed off, sweating and breathless, and the rink rats took over with the scrapers. The Northwesters waited impatiently on the sidelines until a path was cleared around the outer boards. Then, at a word from Red, they sprang to the ice and began skating circuits to warm up.

Pete was on the ice as fast as anyone. "Now!" he said to himself. With the first few cuts of his skates into the ice he felt a kind of elation. He spurted, head-down, purposeful, to the head of the circling band of players and the leaders began going faster to keep up with Pete. Soon they were flying around the ice, yelling at the labouring slower players. Coming up behind Spunska once Pete saw that the big boy was skating a shade better; he was still very rough, but he was taking the corners with more confidence. Pete wondered if Bill could ever catch up to the others, with their casual, unstudied lifetimes of skating.

At another blast from the whistle and a shout from Red, the players picked up their sticks at the bench. Red designated the ones who were to wear the white cotton shirts of the opposition team in the scrimmage, and said, "Pete's line, you start against Hurry Berton's line."

From the time the puck dropped Pete scarcely had a thought except hockey. DeGruchy caught him one hard clean check, but he was up again almost before he touched the ice. He harried opposing forwards behind their own blueline, fed pass after pass to his wings, scored a goal himself when Buchanan passed out of a corner to him. Once, after the lines had been changed, he was fighting in a corner with Pincher Martin for the puck and Pincher's elbow crashed into his teeth and he tasted blood but said nothing and kept on checking, shooting, skating.

Lee Vincent came down to the boards near the end of the hour. The coach stopped where the sportswriter was standing. Turner watched the play closely, hands on hips, his whistle ready in one hand to call offsides, and yelled out the mistakes in his powerful voice.

"Kryschuk! Don't pass the puck without looking!

"Buchanan! If you wanta play right wing maybe Bell will trade, but until then stay on your own wing! If you want to get the puck across shoot it across! That's what the stick's for!"

When he paused, the sportswriter said, "Gordon is going good."

"Yeah," Red said. "Hope he keeps it up."

"Was there any reaction among your kids to that criticism of Gordon on the radio Saturday?"

"Nothing out loud," Red said, still watching

the play. "It seems to have made Gordon go, though."

"I think he would have, anyway."

"Maybe." Then he was yelling at the ice again. "Jamieson! When you get the puck with guys trapped in your own end, get moving! Every one you can leave behind is one you don't have to get by! Don't stop and let them catch you!"

Spunska was away on one of his wild rushes again. But he wasn't quite as clumsy and ineffective this time. He broke fast, his awkwardness seemingly overcome in straight breaks by his real swiftness on his feet. When he got to the opposing defence he tried to swerve with the puck. Head up, he could see little Alec Mitchell barrelling in around the defence from left wing, and just when he lost his balance on the swerve he tried to pass to Mitchell. The idea was right but it was a bad pass, too far ahead. Mitchell reached for it, missed, then had to leap over Spunska's sliding form as he swept across the goalmouth.

When Spunska came back up the ice, digging in clumsily after the play that had spun now to the other end, Red yelled, "Nice try, big boy! That's keeping your head up." And Spunska dug in harder than ever.

"That guy's going to be a hockey player, Red," Lee said.

"I'm going to work him as hard as I can this year in practices," Red said. "If he keeps trying I'll be surprised if he isn't on the team, next year."

"I wouldn't be too surprised to see him get into a game or two this year," Lee said. "You're not exactly overloaded with reserves, you know."

Red grinned. "Don't I know it. But he'll never make it this year."

Then he left the sideboards. He played one side short-handed for a while, and gave pointers on a power play, designed to hem the opposition within their own blueline when they had been penalized. Then he worked on Kryschuk and Wong as penalty-killers for a time when Northwest itself might be short-handed through penalties. He had them rag the puck, pass it back and forth, keep it as long as possible to prevent the side with superiority in numbers from getting it, and then shooting it clear and out of danger at the last instant. Then he had complete forward lines sweep in on defence and told the defencemen how to wait out the play, think it out, feel it out, not get sucked into making a dive at some one player only to have him pass to another in the clear.

In that practice, Pete's line seemed to find itself. He began to catch on to the skating habits of his wingers, the way Buchanan could fly from the blueline and cut around the defence and catch a pass if you could get it to him in front of the goal. He began to realize that Bell was the policeman of the line, that he body-checked hard, more than a forward usually did. He noticed that he couldn't lead Bell too far with a pass, because Bell didn't have Buchanan's quick burst of speed; but that you could yell and lead Buchanan ten feet and he'd get it.

For a minute or two before the end of the practice his line was off, while Berton and Big Canoe and Mitchell took over the harrying of the sweating DeGruchy and Jamieson on defensive drill. When Pete flopped to the bench, by habit now a little way from the others, Bell and Buchanan came over and slumped down beside him.

As Big Canoe scored a goal, Buchanan said, "The Chief is sure going good. That's his third goal."

"Whew!" Bell said. "I'm done. And I thought I was in shape!"

"I'm puffing like a blowtorch," Pete said.

Buchanan said, "You should be, Pete, You were really flying out thēre tonight. We'll show 'em Friday."

Listening to the comradely words, Pete felt good.

CHAPTER 9

On Friday night when Pete reached the Arena the big rink was packed again. Kelvin and Gordon Bell, matched in the first game, were old rivals. They were big schools, only a few blocks apart, and years earlier Gordon Bell had been in the same position as Northwest now – a new school taking the strain from a crowded old one. Since then Gordon Bell had won many honours in high school competition but the students there were never so happy as when they could beat Kelvin.

But, Pete saw, they had nothing to be happy about tonight. By the end of the second period, Kelvin was leading 5–1, showing every sign of a walkaway. He stood by the corridor to the dressing rooms to watch as Keenan and Stimers and the rest of the Kelvin team trooped off grinning at their families and friends who had clustered around to cheer them off the ice. Pete followed the teams to the dressing room. The rink policeman, recognizing him, let him pass without question but stopped the horde of Kelvin boys behind him who would have liked to congratulate their heroes face to face.

Spunska and Fat were the only ones in the dressing room when Pete entered.

"Hi," Pete said, surprised to see Spunska in the room. "Going to play tonight, Bill?"

Spunska shook his head. "I'm helping Fat with the uniforms. He has a lot to do."

Pete noticed the friendly smile Fat and Spunska exchanged, and he said, "You'll make it sooner or later, the way you try."

"What do you think about tonight?" Spunska asked.

Pete shrugged. "Can't tell. They made it tough for Daniel Mac."

"We've got a good chance!" Fat said, stopping in his counting of sweaters.

"Sure," Pete said mildly.

The others began to trickle in soon after the whistle sounded in the corridor to recall the Kelvin and Gordon Bell teams to the ice. They stripped rapidly, and Fat, acting also as trainer, applied tape where necessary. There weren't many strains or bruises, though, this early in the season.

A roar from above signified that the game was going again. Another abrupt roar signified a goal. An outburst of the staccato Kelvin yells told which team had scored it.

"I thought Gordon Bell would fade," De-

Gruchy said. "They really shot their bolt in the second, and even then they couldn't score."

"I was hoping they'd beat Kelvin," Berton said.

"No such luck."

Bell and Buchanan dressed beside Pete, the three of them idly discussing the game above.

Rosario Duplessis came in grinning. "'Allo!" he yelled.

"'Allo, dere!" the others yelled, mimicking him.

Rosy stood in the middle of the floor. "This is a time to be serious!" he yelled. "Now listen 'ere!"

He struck a pose, hands on hips, like the coach often did, and grinned blandly at Red when he looked up from poking in his bag for his skates.

"I have been studying this matter," Rosy said. "This matter of the playoffs." He pronounced it "play-hoffs."

The others were quiet, watching him, waiting for the joke.

"I have looked back," Rosy said. "In the past years any team which gets nine points in the standings, for four times winning and one time tying, gets in the playoffs. Almost always."

"So what?" Bell asked curiously.

"So," said Rosy, "we can afford to lose two

more games out of our eight and still make the playoffs! Isn't that wonderful?"

"Ah-h-h-h, sit down!" the other yelled, laughing.

But Rosy wasn't through. "So three cheers for the playoffs!" he yelled.

In the referee's room, and along the hall, others heard the cheering from Northwest's dressing room and looked at each other, puzzled.

Red, grinning, said, "You're a crazy bird, Rosy!"

But Rosy's joking had seemed to lift them all.

They dressed eagerly, listening to the cheering from the rink. By the time the game was over Kelvin had won 7-2, and as the thumping of skates came down the corridor and the shouts of the Kelvin players sounded, Red stood up in the centre of the dressing room.

"Quiet!" Fat said unnecessarily.

"I'm only going to tell you one thing right now," Red said. "Play your positions. I don't want to see a winger any place but covering his check. This is one of the simplest things in hockey, and seems to be the hardest to remember, but remember it." He paused. "These guys are good, but they can be beaten. Remember that, too. Okay, let's go."

Spunska left first, to get a seat above. Then

Junior Paterson led the team from the dressing room, carrying his big goal stick in one hand and a puck in the other. Pete was close behind him. The roars of the crowd rose and fell around them as they skated out on the ice, and he glanced up into the Northwest section at his parents and Sarah, and then looked again. Spunska was climbing along the aisle to a vacant seat Sarah had been saving beside her. Pete half grinned. He knew that somewhere in the crowd Ron Maclean would be watching that and grumbling to himself.

The coach sent Hurry Berton out first with Big Canoe and Mitchell on the wings, De-Gruchy and lanky Gord Jamieson on defence. On the face-off the St. John's centre got the puck and swept in on defence, and on the bench Pete just had time to think of that game with Kelvin, when Keenan had scored from the first play, when DeGruchy poke-checked the puck away from the St. John's centre and tore down the ice. As he hit the St. John's defence with a crash, a defenceman went down and DeGruchy stayed up. The crowd shouted. Already the fans had shown that nobody could be neutral to one of DeGruchy's electrifying rushes. They either loved him or hated him, and there was nothing in between.

After a minute the coach spoke to Pete and he and Bell and Buchanan rose. Buchanan called to Big Canoe, passing by, and the lines began to change while play was going on, each man on the ice taking any safe opportunity to get off the ice and let his relief go on. Then Pete had the puck and was skating in on defence, head up, placing his wings. He saw Buchanan streaking in on left wing and passed ahead and Buchanan got it but was forced into the corner by the St. John's defenceman. Pete slipped in and stood in front of the goal and Buchanan fought for the puck in the corner and Pete fought to get free of the defence in front of the goal. When the pass came out he got his stick on it and saw a corner open and slapped a backhand at it, but the St. John's goalie kicked it out at the last split second.

Rosy Duplessis and Adam Lawrence had moved up from defence to the St. John's blueline, just a few feet in from the boards. A St. John's defenceman tried to carry the puck out but Duplessis checked him and whooped as he passed across to Lawrence. Lawrence passed into the corner to Henry Bell and Bell tried to carry out in front but was blocked so passed back to the blueline to Rosy, who blazed a shot on goal through the players in front of the net. The crowd went crazy as the puck hit the goal post and came back out to Pete. This jam session isn't over yet, he told them in his mind. Hardly even started!

He worked in on goal but was blocked. He saw Bell in the clear and passed. A desperate St. John's defenceman got his stick on it, and then was checked by Bell in turn. The puck slid to Pete again. He slapped it at the net. Missed the corner by inches. Buchanan fought for the puck behind the goal. Pete twisted free to be ready for the pass. Buchanan tried to slip it around the corner of the net and into the goal. The goalie cleared again. The crowd was going crazier and crazier. St. John's couldn't get the puck out from behind its own blueline, until finally a pass from Bell to Lawrence struck a skate and deflected into the centre zone.

Breakaway! The St. John's centre was on it

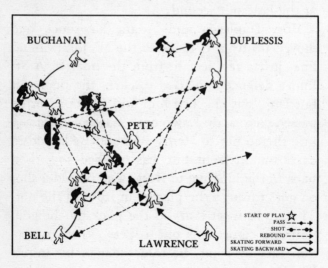

like a flash, Pete after him. Lawrence and Duplessis tried desperately to get back, but they weren't fast enough, and it was a race between Pete and the other centre. Pete closed in foot by foot as the puck carrier crossed the Northwest blueline and just as he straightened away for a shot Pete hooked the puck away from him, made a swooping turn and dashed down centre ice again, the whole Northwest team wheeling to go in with him. He stick-handled across the blueline and again the heat was on; for another mad minute the St. John's goalie was kicking out shot after shot, until finally to relieve the pressure a St. John's defenceman lofted the puck the length of the ice.

The referee's whistle blew at this icing the puck, a rules infraction, and Paterson shot the puck back down the ice for the face-off to the right of the St. John's goal. Pete saw the gate swing open at the Northwest bench and Pincher Martin and Winston Kryschuk and Benny Wong came out. Line change. Defence was changing, too, DeGruchy and Jamieson coming to the ice. Pete didn't even look at DeGruchy as he and Buchanan and Bell skated towards the bench but the crowd burst into warm applause for the remarkable show they'd put on. Pete was puffing hard. On the bench he slumped down and Fat threw a towel around his neck and others around Buchanan and Bell and left them there like scarves.

"That's the way to go!" Red said behind them, and there was a mutter of assent along the bench. . . .

"You really showed 'em, men."

"You were robbed, should've had a goal."

"Should've had three! My gosh!"

Pete turned and grinned at Buchanan and Bell beside him and they grinned back.

"We do that very often," Pete said, "and we'll score."

"I never thought you'd catch that guy, on the breakaway," Buchanan said.

"Neither did I," Pete said.

"Scared me to death," Adam Lawrence said. "I thought, holy cow, we've been murdering them and now they're going to score, instead of us."

Northwest's unexpectedly fierce play seemed to have knocked the St. John's team off balance at first. Near the end of the period they came back strong and bombarded the Northwest goal, but couldn't score. The first period ended scoreless.

The first big break came about halfway through the second. On one of DeGruchy's powerhouse rushes the St. John's defence closed on him too late, and he bashed through and was trying to control the rolling puck to get away a shot when a St. John's winger tripped him from behind and was sent to the penalty box for two minutes. For the next two minutes or until they scored Northwest would have the advantage, St. John's a man short.

The coach sent out Pete's full line with Horatio Big Canoe as an extra forward and DeGruchy the only defenceman. Pete got to the ice stiff-legged with anticipation. This was it!

But the St. John's coach had dreamed up some strategy. He sent a big defenceman to face off with Pete and when the puck was dropped the defenceman simply knocked Pete down with a clean body check and shot the puck down the ice. Pete, up fast, skated back out of the St. John's zone to be onside when the attack formed again. DeGruchy, back for the puck, was checked by a St. John's forward so passed ahead to Big Canoe. The Indian boy cut in to centre, crossed the blueline and stick-handled inside the blueline waiting for his teammates to get into position. Pete pulled up hard in front of the net and Big Canoe blazed a shot at the goal. The goalie stopped it. Pete poked at the rebound but missed. The puck was knocked out to DeGruchy. The big boy fired and Pete, standing just off the corner of the nets, sensed it was going past the side of the goal. He held his stick just off the ice and deflected it into the back corner of the net. The goalie slammed his stick on the ice in disgust and Buchanan and Bell waved their sticks high in the air and yelled, their voices lost in the great sudden roar from the crowd, and they swept down on Pete and clapped him on the back while he skated out to centre ice for the face-off. For the first time in two games, Northwest had a lead, and in the crowd people were looking at each other, pursing their mouths and nodding. A pretty hot underdog, this Northwest.

DeGruchy yelled, "Come on, Hank! Come on, Stretch, boy! Get in there. Let's get a dozen!"

Pete got the draw from the face-off, but lost the puck immediately to a small dark boy who had been sent to the ice, fresh. Pete heard the other St. John's players calling him McMillan. He had uncanny stick-handling ability. He skated towards his own net. The Northwesters followed, puzzled. Jamieson missed with a poke check. Then McMillan turned and swept back, eluded Pete, and skated in a circle in the centre ice zone.

"Check him!" Red yelled from the bench.

DeGruchy lunged. He was an instant too late to prevent McMillan's shot into the Northwest zone. McMillan followed it in, fought valiantly for it with Big Canoe and DeGruchy in a corner and finally held it against the boards with his skate, forcing a face-off.

Lawrence came from the bench to replace DeGruchy and said to Pete, "Red says for two men to check that guy when he hogs the puck that way."

"Tell the Chief," Pete said. While Lawrence told Big Canoe, Pete skated over to Buchanan and Bell to tell them.

But McMillan won the draw, blazed a dangerous shot at the corner of the net, and then buzzed around the Northwest zone like a jet-propelled bumblebee, checking, checking, breaking up plays before they could start.

Back on the bench, Pete held his stick with both hands and dropped his head forward for an instant. For a time his mind was empty of all except elation that Northwest was ahead, and on his goal. But as he got his breath back and watched the play going back and forth on the ice, end to end, he tried to figure out exactly what else it was he felt. He wondered if DeGruchy had noticed. To heck with him, Pete thought. I can get along without him, get along fine.

The bell ended the second period without further scoring. Northwest went to the dressing room for rest, still leading 1-0. The boys flopped on the benches and on the floor, winded, sweating, grinning each time one met another's eyes. This was big. They had a lead. If they could only hold it now.

The coach looked around to see where he was most needed, then went to Junior Paterson down near the showers. Paterson was pale and shaky. Red talked to him soothingly, but he wasn't worried. He'd seen lots of shaky goalkeepers in his life. Most of them lost the shakes as soon as they got back into action. In fact, some of them weren't any good unless they were keyed up this high. While he kept up a running fire of encouragement, he was thinking that goalkeeping was all reflex anyway, no mind could think that fast; dressing room shakes speeded up reflexes, rather than hindered them. So Red wasn't really worried about Paterson. He was thinking about Pete Gordon and Vic DeGruchy.

The way Pete was going tonight made Red feel like a new man. In the first game, only DeGruchy had been able to lift the team, fire the players. Tonight, Pete was firing them, too. Red had seen this immediately. Now he seldom sent Gordon and DeGruchy to the ice at the same time, trying to spread their inspirational play as far as possible. But if they'd only make peace themselves! he thought. My gosh! Two kids, each skating his heart out and they hadn't spoken a word to each other. Wish I could think of a way to fix it. But another game or two like this and they'd just have to tell each other what great guys they are.

Red thought of Rosy and his horseplay about the playoffs. Red could dream, too, although he wouldn't do it out loud, like his players. He was pretty sure right now that Kelvin would be one team in the playoffs. For the other spot, he'd thought probably Daniel Mac. But this St. John's outfit was tough. He grinned. And here we are leading St. John's. Who'd have thought it?

As the whistle blew in the corridor he came back to earth fast. Don't forget there's a period to go, he reminded himself dryly.

"Let's hold 'em this period, kids!" he said. "Let's go."

They charged from the dressing room. And Red saw that DeGruchy and Gordon were walking almost together, and that other players together were clapping each other on the shoulder, talking it up, but not these two. And this would have been a great spontaneous chance for these two mules to call quits to the past. But, Red reflected, it's often the real thoroughbreds who act the most like mules.

Pete's line started the third period. Immediately he noticed that the St. John's coach had changed his strategy. Facing Pete was McMillan. He seemed to have been ordered to check Pete, nothing else, hold that hot Gordon from scoring. Pete got the draw, but McMillan stayed with him, slapping at the puck, until

Pete lost it. And then in the next minute or two he knew what it was to be tied up. Every time he relaxed, McMillan was all over him. He seemed to be watching always for times when Pete was off balance or unawares. Pete was more disgusted than hurt. He caught a grin on McMillan's face.

Bell, Pete's hard-rock right winger, turned angrily to Red the next time they came to the bench, after almost everybody on the St. John's team had thrown a body check at Pete.

"Next time out," he said, "every time somebody knocks down Pete, I'm going to knock the guy into the cheap seats!"

"Don't!" Pete said, without looking up. "That's what they're trying to do, make me mad or make somebody else mad enough to get a penalty. Don't fall for it." He was bruised but cool. He was okay.

"What Pete says is right, Henry," Red said. "Don't let them suck you in. . . . How you going, Pete? You're taking a lot of punishment."

"I'm fine."

On the ice again, McMillan's face, across from Pete in the face-off, was tense. It was all very well to tie up Pete Gordon, but they had to get that goal back, too. McMillan got the draw, and drove in on the Northwest goal. Pete got the puck on a sweep check with his stick and McMillan, turning, saw Bell with his head down, unaware, and dealt him a ferocious, but legal, body check. Bell hit the ice hard but was up again fast, trying to catch up on the play. Pete got a shot on goal. McMillan came up with the rebound and started back up the ice, swerving, Pete after him. Pete saw Bell going for McMillan from his wing. Bell's eyes were cold, calculating. McMillan saw him coming too, and took advantage of it. The instant Bell hit him, he passed to the wing Bell should have been covering. The boy was away like the wind. Rosy missed on a body check and the winger took one look at the goal situation and fired a low shot at the wide side. Paterson's splits across the net were a second too late. The game was tied.

Red called the line in immediately. Skating over, Pete knew that despite his warning, and Red's warning, Bell had let his resentment get him until McMillan became a person, a person to get, instead of just a fast-moving digit that Pete could handle by himself. But that was the game. Any game that moved this fast and hit this hard could never be played to set rules of conduct. People just weren't built that way.

But his head snapped up when DeGruchy, getting off the bench, growled at Bell, "You darn fool, losing your head! Might've cost us the . . ."

He never got a chance to finish. Pete wheeled on him, white-hot. "Shut up!"

DeGruchy's face flushed dark red.

"Bell's playing as hard a game as you or anyone else!" Pete said. There was all the resentment of two weeks behind his anger. "Get out there and get the goal back and shut up! Everybody makes mistakes! Even you."

"Hey!" Red called. "Can that, there!"

In the general excitement of the goal, the fans, except for those close by the bench, hadn't noticed the exchange. Pete pushed through angrily to the bench. DeGruchy looked at him again. Then, his face set hard, he skated to his defence position. Red had sent out Pincher Martin's line, and they fought like wildcats to get the goal back but couldn't. Then Berton's line had a shot at it, and finally Pete's line came out, well rested, with ten minutes of the period left. By this time DeGruchy and Jamieson had had another rest and were back on, too. And it was from a face-off near the Northwest blueline that it happened.

Pete got the draw, evaded a check from McMillan and outskated him in the centre zone, but when he crossed the blueline both Buchanan and Bell were too well covered to take a pass. So he didn't pass, but swerved inside the blueline hoping one of them could work into the clear. Then McMillan hit him from the side and bounced him into a St. John's defenceman coming up from the other side and Pete for an instant was sandwiched crushingly between the two. He felt as if he'd been hit by a train on one side and knocked into a stone wall on the other side. As Pete went down Bell hit the St. John's defenceman, and the boy was thrown on top of Pete in a mêlée of skates and sticks. Pete felt a stunning blow on his left leg below the knee.

McMillan got the puck and was away, with both his wings. Buchanan and Bell had been caught flat-footed deep in the St. John's zone. Only Jamieson was back, but DeGruchy got back fast and broke up the play. St. John's kept it in the Northwest zone.

Bell and Buchanan sped in and covered their checks, while Pete got up, shaken. His left foot seemed numb. When he tried to speed down to cover McMillan he felt the first terrible stabbing pain in his leg. He put his head down and dug in but his leg wouldn't work properly, and as if in a dream he saw McMillan pass to a wing and then drive in to the front of the goal unchecked because he, Pete, couldn't get to him. Half bent over, struggling, fighting the flashing pain that had replaced the numbness, Pete tried to get there in time. The pass came out to McMillan in front of the net. He trapped the puck uncovered. Pete was ten feet away, eight feet, and just as McMillan shot Pete dove headlong with his stick out and caught enough of the puck so that it was deflected upward over the net and the screen, into the crowd.

He lay on the ice, and DeGruchy was the first to see the blood.

He threw aside his stick and gloves and kneeled beside Pete. Without a word he put his hands under Pete's shoulders and pulled him up until he was sitting on the ice. Fat and Red Turner were slip-slipping across the ice rapidly towards them, and Pete, dazed, saw the blood that had soaked his stocking and stained the side of his boot and was forming a red blotch on the white ice. That pile-up, that blow on his leg, it must have been a skate. . . .

"Gosh!" DeGruchy said. "You saved a sure goal, Pete. There's a trail of it right back to where you got hit." DeGruchy's words seemed to be coming hard. "I'll help you up."

Red was there, and Fat. They took a look at the leg and Red took one arm, DeGruchy the other, and they lifted Pete. He tried to stand on his bad leg, but it rebelled violently.

"Better get him to the dressing room," Red said. "Fat, you go to Box F and make sure the doc comes right down."

The rink was quiet, as always after an injury, then hand-clapping for Pete began as the little procession went towards the dressing room, Pete sliding on one skate, the tip of his left skate touching the ice with no weight on it. When they got to the gate, Red called Adam Lawrence over.

"You help him in there, Adam. Hurt much, Pete?"

Pete said, through tight teeth, "It'll be okay." He was thinking of DeGruchy kneeling beside him on the ice, of DeGruchy's words, really the first friendly words spoken between them.

Lawrence took over from Red, and Fat, back with the young doctor who watched all these games from a box near the dressing room passage, took the other side. But as Pete stepped off the ice, DeGruchy touched him again from behind. Pete turned.

"Hope you're back soon," DeGruchy said in a harsh, strained voice.

Red, looking from one to the other, waited another few seconds. He knew this was an important time for his team, and he wanted it cleaned up now, and he wanted them both to say everything they wanted to say, in this moment of stress and emotion.

DeGruchy said, "Pete, I'm sorry. I guess I didn't understand. I'm a dope."

"Better get him down there," the doctor said.

For a few seconds Pete fought with himself. His feeling against DeGruchy was so strong that it couldn't all go at once, and just because he'd been hurt. Heck, did a guy have to shed blood to get on the right side of DeGruchy? But DeGruchy was as stubborn in this, apparently, as in anything. He said, almost pleading for an answer now, "We're okay now, eh, Pete?"

Finally, it was okay. "Sure. . . . We're okay, Grouchy. We'll murder the bums."

They grinned at each other, taut pale grins, both of them.

Then Fat and Lawrence and the doctor took Pete to the dressing room.

Pete breathed deeply on the frosty air, the pain coming in waves.

"My car's been sitting," the doctor said. "It'll be too cold. We'll take a cab."

He beckoned to one waiting by the rink door and helped Pete into the front seat and asked the driver to turn his heater on full. He took Pete's clothes from Fat and as the driver was about to pull away Fat said hurriedly, "Gee, you played a great game, Pete. Hope you're back soon."

DeGruchy, and then Fat. Funny how one game can change things. As the taxi made a quick turn toward the nearby street Pete saw through the closing rink door that Sarah was hurrying out. He saw Fat stop her. He'd be explaining what all had happened.

But it wasn't until much later that Pete really knew himself all that had happened. It started the next morning, after they'd listened to the radio account of how Northwest suddenly crumbled after he left and St. John's scored three times to win 4-1. Pete was telling his parents and Sarah at breakfast about going to the hospital, about the doctor giving a local anaesthetic, and then putting six stitches into the cut to close it. He'd been too tired, when his dad drove him home last night from the hospital, to say much.

The phone rang. Sarah went to answer it, then returned. "For you, Pete."

Pete went to the phone, in the hall. "Hello," he said.

"Pete?"

"Yes."

"This is Elmer McMillan from St. John's Tech."

Pete smiled. "I can't even get away from you at breakfast time, eh?"

McMillan chuckled, but sounded embarrassed. "I just called to see how your leg is."

"It's not bad," Pete said. "I'll miss our game with Daniel Mac next week, darn it, but the next week we're not playing and I'll be back for the game with Gordon Bell on the twentieth, the doc says."

"Gosh, I'm sorry," McMillan said. "I mean, I was supposed to be checking you hard, but I hate to see anybody hurt."

"It was a clean check," Pete said. "Nothing wrong about it. Just an accident. Forget it."

"Well, I'm glad you feel that way."

"We'll beat you next time, to get even," Pete said.

McMillan didn't comment on that, but he said, "It wasn't like the same team after you left. . . . But I won't keep you. I just wanted to tell you I'm sorry."

"Thanks for calling," Pete said. "See you."

"So long."

After breakfast, Pete limped into the living room. He could scarcely stand on his leg this morning. It was stiff and sore. He stretched out on the couch and was listening to the radio when the doorbell rang.

"I'll get it!" Sarah called, hurrying from the kitchen.

Pete heard her voice, surprised. "Oh, hello. . . ."

"How's Pete?" It was Fat's voice.

"Come in and see him. He's downstairs."

"No. I can't. I just brought these, case he wants to read them. Hope he's better soon."

Pete heard retreating footsteps on the veranda, then down the steps, and Sarah came smiling into the room with a bundle of papers.

"Fat?" Pete asked.

She was smiling. "Yes. He just shoved these at me and ran." She looked at them. "Looks like all winter's issues of the *Hockey News*."

Pete sat quietly for a few seconds. All a guy had to do was try, and Fat was his friend. He picked up the top paper and started looking at the pictures, leafing through them until he found feature stories about big-league players.

He was deep in a story about his favourite big-league centreman, Bryan Trottier of the

Islanders, when the doorbell rang again. Before he thought, he rose. He winced at the pain, but now that he was up he continued to the door. It was DeGruchy. Behind him, parked on the street, was a panel delivery truck. On the side was the sign DEGRUCHY'S GROCERIES AND FINE MEATS. DeGruchy was dressed in clothes rougher than those he wore to school, a pair of thick woollen pants tucked into high leather boots, a Mackinaw coat with a sheepskin collar, big leather gauntlets, a ski cap with the ear flaps down. The relief on DeGruchy's big tough face was almost funny.

"Boy, am I glad to see you up!" he said.

"Come on in," Pete said.

Vic stepped into the vestibule after knocking snow from his boots. "I'm helping my dad today, delivering. Thought I'd see how you were."

Sarah came from the kitchen, where she'd been helping with the breakfast dishes, greeted DeGruchy with unmistakable surprise, mixed with relief, and went on upstairs.

"I'm out for two weeks, according to the doc," Pete said.

There was an awkward silence, and then DeGruchy put his hand on the doorknob, and his eyes met Pete's. "We'll be real tough when you get back."

Then he almost bolted out of the door.

In the next week, at school, Pete found he had a hundred friends where he hadn't seemed to have any before. Girls smiled at him shyly as he limped through the halls, and at lunchtime in the cafeteria his table was always crowded with other members of the team. Teachers asked him solicitously how his leg was coming along, and he had to tell dozens of times the doctor's verdict that he was out for two weeks. Henry Bell even took to bringing his old car to school so he could drive Pete home. It was a funny week, so different from the week before. But when the doctor took the stitches out on Wednesday, he still insisted that Pete was to keep out of this game with Daniel Mac.

On the night of the game, Pete's father had a bad cold and couldn't go, and his mother stayed home, too. So Pete drove the car through the lightly falling snow to the rink, Sarah with him. They met Spunska in the lobby. The three of them got seats together in the midst of the cheering, happy-go-lucky throng.

Pete wasn't patient. When the teams were warming up, Pete itched to be out there. He thought of little things he knew about the Daniel Mac plays which would come in handy if he were playing against them.

But the shuffle in the lineup caused by Pete's absence was felt early. At first Red played the

Berton and Martin lines turnabout, using Pete's wings as penalty-killers in a rough first period. But the two overworked forward lines began to tire perceptibly under the heavy bumping of the Daniel Macs, so Red moved Rosy Duplessis up from defence to centre Pete's line. But this left him with only three defencemen.

DeGruchy played a magnificent game. On his first rush when he was hit by Ron Maclean at the Daniel Mac defence the sound of impact could be heard right up in the top seats. Both went down. The first time Maclean made a rush, DeGruchy gave back that tough check, with interest, and from then through the game these two supplied a side show that had the crowd on its feet in expectancy every time one approached the other. DeGruchy got the first real results about halfway through the period by setting up a play that Berton finished beautifully, drawing out the Daniel Mac goalie to score for Northwest. But Maclean got it back on a drive from the blueline through a maze of players. The first period ended in a 1-1 tie.

But in the second period the roof fell in. DeGruchy was penalized for grabbing the puck with his hands in a pile-up in front of the Northwest net, and while he was off Daniel Mac scored. Later in the period they got more goals to lead 5-1. In the third Northwest recovered briefly for two, then Daniel Mac scored four more without a reply. The game ended 9-3 for Daniel Mac.

After a debate, Sarah and Bill and Pete decided to stay for the Gordon Bell game with St. John's, although they all felt it would be a one-sided victory for St. John's. They were wrong. The Gordon Bells played way above the form they'd showed in their first game with Kelvin and scored in the last minute of play to beat St. John's 3-2.

On the way out of the rink, Pete said, "I wish Gordon Bell had stayed bad long enough for us to play them. One win under our belt and we might start going all right."

"Maybe we'll beat them anyway," Bill said.

"Sure we will," said Sarah.

They were outside in the crowd now and the light snow still was falling. Boys and girls from victorious Gordon Bell and Daniel Mac shattered the night with their war cries. Limping along, Pete thought suddenly of Bill getting up early every morning, when it was still dark, going down to a cold rink, turning on just enough lights to see, and then skating by himself.

"What time do you have to get up, to get to the rink at six?"

"Five o'clock."

"I'll bet your mother loves that!" Pete said.

"Oh, surely she doesn't get up, too?" Sarah asked.

In the light of a streetlight they were passing, Bill suddenly looked unhappy. "She would like to, but she's sick."

"Oh, I didn't know!" Sarah said quickly. "Is it a cold or something like that?"

Bill said, "I guess it's everything that's happened, all piled up. The doctor said she's had a real rest coming to her for years and maybe this is it."

The three of them were silent the rest of the way to the car. Gosh, what a guy this Spunska is, Pete was thinking. . . . New country, mother sick, and he's trying harder than anybody I ever knew to be a hockey player.

He insisted on driving Bill home. The Spunskas lived several blocks north of the Gordons, in an older part of the city, near the railroad yards. Once the railway had built a street of houses for yard workers. Since, they'd been sold. They were all the same, row after row of joined verandas, on narrow lots.

"That's it," Bill said, pointing.

Although in architecture, or lack of it, the house was the same as all the others, it stood out from the rest. The walk had been shovelled recently, the veranda and steps swept.

"Please come in," Bill said. "I would like you to meet my father. And my mother too, if she's awake."

"But if she's sick . . ." Sarah began.

"If you think it's all right," Pete said quickly, feeling that Bill wouldn't have asked them in unless he really wanted to. He parked the car and they walked up the walk.

Bill opened the door for them. The vestibule was small and cramped, but neat. It led directly into a small living room. While Pete was taking off his overshoes, he could see a man, tall and thin, rising from a chair, putting down a book. Bill introduced them to his father.

"How is Mother?" Bill asked.

Mr. Spunska shrugged, and a worried look crossed his face. "She is about the same." He had a heavy accent.

A weak voice from upstairs said, "Come to see me, Bill. Bring up your friends."

"Would you?" Bill asked Pete and Sarah.

They went upstairs. The stairs had been painted recently, and so had the floor above. Bill led them into a small bedroom, almost filled by a large double bed. In it was a woman with a thin face, huge dark eyes, black hair drawn back severely from her forehead.

"You are Pete and Sarah," she said, her voice almost a whisper. "Bill has told me. . . ." They said hello, and that they were sorry she was sick, then there was a silence. She seemed very weak.

"We lost tonight, Mother," Bill said.

"That is too bad," she whispered. "I am glad you brought your friends home with you. Now go and have something to eat." She mustered a smile. "I hope to see you again, many times," she said to Pete and Sarah. "Soon now I will be better. This staying in bed . . ." She shook her head sadly.

Bill signalled and they left the room quietly, Pete thinking of the sort of satisfaction that had shown on Mrs. Spunska's face when she said she was glad Bill had brought his friends home. . . .

Mr. Spunska had coffee ready, and sandwiches. They sat around the scarred dining room table. Pete and Sarah felt uneasy at first, but quickly warmed to Bill's father.

It took Mr. Spunska – Pete didn't know yet whether to call him Mister, or Professor, or what – a while to say anything. But when he began, in his heavily accented voice, he was a nice guy. He joshed Bill about his ambition to be an athlete, and spoke of the university, and soon drew Pete and Sarah into conversation about what courses they hoped to take in college, and why.

"I hope to be a lawyer," Pete said.

"And you?" he asked Sarah.

"Psychology," she said.

He joked, "To be a good wife, eh? A greater ambition than some."

Driving home, Sarah said, "Nice people."

Thoughtfully, Pete said, "They sure have it tough, don't they?"

And the next morning while it was still dark, he wakened suddenly, wide awake although he had had only five or six hours' sleep. He looked at the luminous dial of his alarm. Five-thirty. Bill would be making his breakfast so he could get down to the rink. Pete lay for a minute thinking that if he just tried, he could get back to sleep. Then he got up, turned on his light, and dressed swiftly. He could be back by the time Dad needed the car. He tested his leg. It was still a little stiff. But it would do, if he took it easy. . . .

He stayed in the car, in front of the rink, to put on his skates because he knew it would be warmer there than inside. Bill's bike stood against the door, but the front of the rink was dark and lonely. When Pete got out of the car, carrying an old and battered hockey stick he'd found in the basement, relic of another year, the frost was sharp and the snow crunched under foot. He couldn't explain the excitement he felt.

Inside, in the hollow quiet, he could hear the reverberating slap of a puck against the boards. He walked across the long lobby and quietly opened one of the doors to the ice.

Bill, in a ski cap, several sweaters, his pants

tucked into a pair of department store hockey stockings, was winding up behind one of the goals. He charged awkwardly down the ice pushing a puck before him through a maze of nail kegs set at intervals on the ice. He lost the puck, crashed into one of the kegs, recovered without falling, picked up the puck again, skated directly at a nail keg and tried to swerve at the last possible instant, but fell down. Then he was up again, chasing the puck, turning to his right and then to his left.

Pete had a lump in his throat. Spunska hadn't noticed him. A clock in a nearby church struck the quarter-hour. Six-fifteen. Through the top windows were the stars of night. And Spunska skated, fell, rose again, trying to weave with the puck through the nail kegs. Quite an idea, setting up his own obstacles so he'd have to learn to wheel and turn quickly. Pete threw one leg over the boards and dropped to the ice.

He yelled at Spunska, a high happy yell. He laughed aloud when he saw the utter surprise on the big boy's face.

"Come on, Bill!" he yelled. "Skate! You've got a lot to learn. Let's go, boy!"

It was a minute or two later when the two boys noticed the two men who had entered the rink only a minute or two behind Pete – Lee Vincent of the *Telegram*, with a very sleepy-looking photographer.

CHAPTER 11

Pete sat in the dressing room at the Arena. The room was in the chaotic state of fifteen minutes before game time. Some players were yelling for tape or shoelaces and the rest were yelling to each other just for the sheer excitement of it. The smashing defeat by Daniel Mac seemingly was forgotten. Tonight the target was Gordon Bell.

"What an outfit this is!" Pete said, grinning, to Fat, who was passing out gum.

"They're glad you're back," Fat said, and passed on. He was in a hurry. Even if he'd had eight arms, he couldn't have handled all the requests he was getting.

It had been funny with Fat, these last two weeks. The skinny little guy had been so hostile at first. And now he'd do anything for Pete. Everybody on the team was a hero to Fat, but if he considered any above the rest, obviously they were Pete and Grouchy DeGruchy. Pete grinned at the way Fat scampered around trying to keep him happy now, and yet it made him feel warm inside. Fat was the kind of a guy you wanted to do things for, because he appreciated them so much.

Red came up and stood in front of Pete. "You're really sure that leg is set to go, eh?" he asked.

Pete nodded. "Hardly feel it now."

The morning sessions at the rink had helped, the hours spent with Spunska and DeGruchy. Yes, DeGruchy! Pete still couldn't get over that. That first morning he'd gone down there by chance had been the one Lee Vincent had chosen to get his material for a feature story on the Polish boy, Spunska, who was trying so hard to catch up on a lifetime of skating practice that he'd missed.

Pete could remember parts of Lee's story, about how he'd been tipped off by Petersen, the rink manager, about Spunska's predawn workouts, had gone to the rink expecting to find the boy alone, and instead had found that Pete Gordon, the boy some people believed was Northwest's problem child, still with a very bad leg, had turned out to help Spunska catch up on the rest of Canadian boys.

The story had appeared in Monday's paper. When Pete went to the sports office at school the next day at noon most of the team was gathered there discussing it. And DeGruchy had said, "Say, Pete, I could help. I don't know too much about playing defence myself, but what I know I could tell him." And he'd been there on Wednesday morning, and every morning since.

The three boys had sat together at last Friday's doubleheader. Northwest didn't play. Daniel Mac beat Gordon Bell 4-1 and then Kelvin came from behind to edge St. John's Tech 6-5. But the game had been costly for Kelvin. Barker, the big defenceman, broke a wrist in a pile-up along the boards and would be out for a month anyway.

Now, sitting in the dressing room, Pete ran over the league standings in his mind. Kelvin had won all three of its games and led the league with six points. Daniel Mac was second with five points for two wins and a tie; St. John's third with a win, a tie, and two defeats; Gordon Bell fourth with a win and two losses. Northwest was in the basement. Three games. Three losses.

Pete got to his feet and walked nervously around the floor. They had to start tonight. Funny. He knew down inside that man for man, against other teams, Northwest shouldn't win any games. It was this amazing spirit, which now had rubbed off on him, too, that made him feel not particularly that they *should* win, but that they couldn't be beaten.

Everybody was ready now. Junior Paterson

waddled across the floor in his heavy goal equipment and stood beside Pete. He was eating a chocolate bar.

"You'll get fat, Junior," Pete said.

"Couldn't eat any supper, darn it," Junior said.

"Nervous?"

"You bet."

"Me, too."

The two boys sat down in the sudden quiet, everybody ready now, waiting for the word from Red to go up to the ice to warm up.

"I wonder if a guy ever stops being nervous before a game," Junior said, nibbling half-heartedly on his chocolate.

Red, big hands in his jacket pockets, eyes nervous with tension, overheard the words. "When he does," the coach said, "he's usually no good any more as a hockey player. I've seen guys who manage to learn how to hide being nervous, but they were nervous all the same. There was one we had in Toronto who used to boast that he never felt nervous. Somebody broke a light bulb in the dressing room one night, sounded like a shot, and the guy didn't stop shaking for ten minutes."

The coach walked into the middle of the floor. "All right," he said. "Everybody ready?"

The words were scarcely out of his mouth when Paterson, who was closest to the door, yanked it open. The players stampeded into the empty corridor and in a few seconds they were on the ice. The Northwest section greeted them with boisterous cheering. Cheerleaders of other schools, responding to the challenge, whipped their constituents into a rolling barrage of noise.

Pete bowed his head suddenly when, in a few seconds of quiet, somebody in the Northwest section yelled, "What's the matter with Gordon?"

And the reply was a bellow: "HE'S ALL RIGHT!"

He picked up the puck, skated through the centre zone, and fired a long shot in on goal. Then he lined up with the others on the blueline. Grouchy dashed in on goal and Paterson took his hard shot on his pads. Adam Lawrence, in the corner, shot it back out to Pete, who took a try on goal, and they kept this up, taking turns testing Paterson, until the whistle blew for the first face-off at centre ice.

Pete skated off the ice. Red started the Berton line against Gordon Bell's top line, three little speedsters called Bush, Bevan and Jones. Pete took a seat on the bench near the gate, with Bell and Buchanan beside him.

"I hope these guys are having one of their bad nights," Stretch Buchanan said.

"We'll take 'em anyway," Fat said.

Pete was thinking of what Stretch had said. It was true. This season Gordon Bell either had been very good or very bad. The night they were whammed 7-2 by Kelvin they looked as if they couldn't beat their way out of a cloud of smoke, but the next week they'd come back and played a terrific game to beat the strong St. John's outfit, 3-2. Then they'd looked bad against Daniel Mac. Heck, the Daniels could have scored ten goals if they hadn't been so erratic around the net, but Gordon Bell had seemed even worse. They were a skating team, perhaps the fastest team in the league, man for man. Pete grinned when he remembered the criticism Grouchy had delivered the night they lost to Daniel Mac.

"Those guys!" Grouchy had said, in disgust. "Open the gate at the end of the rink and they'd skate four miles straight north before anybody looked to see where they were going!"

A whistle! The puck dropped! Berton snared it and was checked immediately. The little Gordon Bell winger, Jones, got the puck behind his own defence and went down right wing like a rocket, but was going so fast that when he cut in around the defence he wound up behind the Northwest net and Grouchy had the puck.

Pete watched DeGruchy rush. It made his spine tingle to watch. Grouchy wasn't a good skater. He wasn't a good stick-handler, either. If you took him apart to analyse him, you'd have to come right down to it, he was all drive, all spirit. . . . Holding his stick in one hand, pushing the puck along in front of him, he crossed his own blueline, then the centre red line, head up, watching the pattern of the defence forming against him, watching his own team for chances to make a good pass, his hair flying out behind him, his big flat face intent and menacing. The crowd roared in a rising shout. He evaded a check, bashed his way across the Gordon Bell blueline, charged into the defence, passed at the last instant to Horatio Big Canoe. The Chief drove in for a hard shot. The goalie caught it and tossed it away, while DeGruchy dug in back down the ice to get into position to stem the return rush.

"What a guy!" Pete said.

"And he said he couldn't have made the Daniel Mac team!" Buchanan said. "He's crazy. No class at all, but you can't stop him."

"There isn't a team I ever saw that he couldn't make," Pete said. "And that's the truth."

"Get on there, Pete!" Red said behind him.

Pete yelled at Hurry Berton. Berton shot the puck at the Gordon Bell goal and hopped over the boards. Pete was on. The Chief and Mitch got to the bench seconds later and then Pete was at centre, ranging in a short circle to get up speed and then he was stride for stride with the

Gordon Bell centre, batting away a pass. His leg, apart from brief twinges of pain, didn't bother him; it didn't slow him up at all. He got the puck in a corner and was surrounded. Holding his stick with a short grip in his right hand, he dragged the puck out of the corner, using his left hand to fend off checkers, push other sticks out of the way. In six feet he was in stride, flying, cutting in to centre to place his wings properly, and now he had both hands on his stick and laid across a perfect pass to Bell, who cut in on the Gordon Bell defence.

But, it was apparent now, this was one of Gordon Bell's good nights. A big boy with a handsome but sullen face was playing a whale of a game on defence. Pete watched him check Buchanan and he thought Stretch was going to break in half at the jolt.

"Attaboy, Forsyth!" Bush yelled beside him. "That's hitting him, Buck, boy!"

Then Bush was away with the puck, Pete after him. Lawrence checked Bush, passed to Pete, and then Pete was weaving in on Forsyth. He was crowded by Bush, couldn't shift. He passed. Forsyth hit him, and as Pete was going down Forsyth cross-checked him heavily with his stick, although he was already down and out of the play.

"Hey, can that!" Pete yelped, getting up.

"Can't take it, eh, big shot?" Forsyth said. He

had a mean look on his face. But mean or not, sullen or not, he was a hard guy to get around.

On the next player change Red came along the bench behind Pete's line and said, "These guys are hot tonight. Don't let anybody let himself get caught out of position." Pete heard him passing the same word along the bench.

For the rest of the first period Northwest played it cagey, checking hard, hoping for a break. Pete marvelled sometimes that the Gordon Bells didn't score. His line could skate with them, but Berton's line was a little slower, except for the Chief. The Martin line was clearly outclassed in everything but results. Somehow, Martin and Wong and Kryschuk managed to bump the faster Gordon Bell wingers often enough to keep them off stride, and Martin himself was a star, stick-handling with all the wizardry of years on the corner rinks, breaking up play after play with his long poke check. The first period ended without either side scoring, and both teams, grim now, quiet with the knowledge that this was as tough a game as they'd ever find, slumped on the benches to rest.

Between periods, Pete could hear from above the rising and falling cadences of a song, sung to the tune of "My Bonnie Lies Over the Ocean." After it was sung, there were cheers and boos from above. And then followed the

Northwest yell. When they got back to the ice for the second period, their appearance was heralded by this song again, and Pete saw it was from the Northwest section. All the Northwest players stood on the ice, listening, grinning to each other at the words ringing out:

> *Oh, Northwest is now in the basement,*
> *No victories so far have we,*
> *But we're not in last place forever,*
> *Not we! Oh, not we! Oh, not we!*

Pete and Grouchy stood together at the blueline. Pete could see Spunska and Sarah singing, and his mother and father smiling beside them.

"Some guy on the student athletic association made it up," Grouchy said. "There were copies passed around when the people were coming in tonight. Good, eh?"

"They'll have to change the words, though," Pete said. "Maybe even after tonight."

"Yeah." Pete and Grouchy looked at each other and grinned.

The cheerleaders for other schools looked almost ludicrously downcast, listening to the song. Northwest, whatever its position in the league, was the only school with a spur-of-the-moment song.

The second period was as close as the first. Check, check, check. Skate, skate, skate. Grouchy handed out some crushing body checks, trying to slow down the Gordon Bell speedsters, but they recovered fast. After fourteen minutes of the second period Grouchy got a penalty. His long sweep check at Bush, the Gordon Bell centre, missed the puck and got Bush's skates and the little fellow went down and the referee waved Grouchy off, two minutes for tripping.

Then Gordon Bell really turned on the heat. Red sent out Pincher Martin and Pete to try to kill off the penalty, because they were two of the best stick-handlers on the team. But with Grouchy off the defence, Gordon Bell got the puck into the Northwest zone and set up a pattern passing play with two men on the blueline, one at each side, two men in the corners, and one fighting for room in front of the net. Northwest, with only four defenders to cover these five men, couldn't get the puck. Every time they got close, the Gordon Bell player would pass to the one man who always had to be uncovered, and finally it paid off. A pass came out to centre and Forsyth, the big defenceman, fired a blazing shot through a maze of legs and skates and sticks. Paterson never saw it until it was past him, into the net.

Northwest stormed around the Gordon Bell net trying to score. Grouchy, back on the ice, made rush after rush. Berton missed a heartbreaker. The Gordon Bell goalkeeper was sprawled across the goalmouth and Hurry, who had to shoot over him, fired too high, over the top of the net.

In the last minutes of the second period, and the early part of the third, Gordon Bell defended desperately and well. Northwest gradually opened up, trying to get back the goal. Paterson, who had spent the rest between the second and third blaming himself over and over for missing that screened shot, made two stupendous stops on clean breakaways. Grouchy was on the ice most of the time, and even when he was on the bench he was nagging Red all the time to get back on.

He and Forsyth had a brief exchange. Forsyth checked Martin hard along the boards, and there was no penalty. Grouchy complained to the referee but, as usual, that was a waste of breath. So Grouchy took it into his own hands. The next time he carried the puck he went in on Forsyth's side and knocked the big boy flying. The next time Grouchy rushed, Forsyth kept out of the way.

"He just likes hitting the little guys," Grouchy puffed to Pete before a face-off a few seconds later.

But Northwest was still behind. The minutes ticked by on the big clock that hung down at centre ice. Four minutes left to play in the game. Three. Two. And then came what looked like a back-breaking penalty. Grouchy got it again. On one of his rushes he passed and then took two or three steps before he knocked down a Gordon Bell defender, and the referee called it charging, and it was. Grouchy argued and slammed his stick down on the ice and the referee gave him a misconduct penalty for arguing. It didn't mean much right now, as he was off for the rest of the game anyway.

The Gordon Bell players yelled at each other with glee when Grouchy was put off. The face-off was just outside the Gordon Bell blueline and Red, with nothing to lose, pulled off both defencemen and put on Pete, Berton, Big Canoe and Martin. When they were milling around, before the face-off, the four Northwest players came together and Pete had a sudden desperate plan.

"Look, you guys," he said. "Always one of us hang around centre ice. They're bound to get it into our end, with five players against four, but one of us always hang around the red line and the other watch for a chance to pass for a breakaway."

The others nodded. Martin took the face-off. Pete stood a few feet behind him, tense, waiting. This long pass up to the red line was a good breakaway play when one side was trapped in the other's end, but it was dangerous when the side contemplating it was shorthanded, because it meant the man at the red line was out of checking action, leaving five attackers against only three defenders and the goalie. And Pete knew it had to work the first time. After that, if Gordon Bell saw that this was the plan, they'd leave the man back themselves to watch the man loitering at centre.

Martin lost the draw and with a shout the Gordon Bell team was away, trying to clinch the game with another goal. The passes went back and forth down the ice, Martin and the Chief and Berton trying to break it up, and Pete made one check and then, seeing that the others were going in, he stayed back at the red line, crouching, skating as if he were hurt a little, and slow on that account.

Paterson stopped one shot, got the rebound, batted it out to a Gordon Bell player's stick, stopped that shot, too, and the crowd was going wild. Pete knew that if Gordon Bell scored again people would be asking him why he wasn't in there checking with the rest.

But then Martin got the puck! He tried to get it out, lost it. But Berton got it. He looked up and saw Pete.

The instant Pete saw that glance he circled so that he'd be moving fast when the pass came out. He was. The pass was flat and perfect and hit his stick just as he picked up speed at centre ice.

Everybody in the rink jumped up, yelling, as

Pete broke for the Gordon Bell goal. Nobody back. And he was thinking, this is our only chance, don't shoot too soon, don't shoot too late, make the goalie move first. He sped in, head up, the instinctive feel of the puck at the end of his stick, and he heard the skate cuts behind him as the Gordon Bells came back desperately, flying, and then he faked a shot at the right side of the net and the goalie didn't move and on the fly he blasted desperately at a tiny opening on the short side of the net. . . . It was in!

He lay on the ice under Forsyth, who had hit him just as he shot. From the noise, he thought the rink was falling down; there were tears of joy in his eyes and his throat was full, because he had done it right. And then Berton and Martin and the Chief were hauling Forsyth off, roughly, dragging Pete to his feet, rumpling his hair, yelling, and he looked up at the clock and saw that only eight seconds remained in the game. He stayed on for the face-off. He got it, and passed to Martin, and Martin was still stick-handling in the centre zone when the buzzer ended the game.

The crowd overflowed to the ice. Rink policemen ran this way and that trying to herd the yelling, cheering, singing Northwest fans back to their seats. The Northwest players from the bench mobbed Pete. Paterson shoved through the crowd and put his arms around Pete and just about crushed him with a big hug. Grouchy jumped out of the penalty box, and had his arm around Pete's shoulders as they pushed through the crowd. Spunska was on the other side, opening a hole for Pete through the throng. In the dressing room, with the door locked behind them, the celebration continued as the players stripped down in a hurry and showered and dressed. Fat walked around putting things into the wrong trunks, rubbing his face dazedly. Spunska, his face one big grin, helped him. Red stood in the middle of the floor and muttered to himself, grinning, "If this is what happens when we tie one, I wonder what'll happen if we ever win?"

CHAPTER 12

The only day in the next two weeks that Pete and Grouchy and Spunska missed opening the door at the old rink by six in the morning was Christmas. In the Gordon household, Christmas always was celebrated with a big tree and a family gathering around it before breakfast on Christmas Day, to receive presents. Pete could scarcely keep his eyes off the wrist watch his mother and father had bought for him, his first really good one, but even more amazing was that Sarah had knitted him a cardigan – and it fitted! There'd been no clue that she was making something for him. There were many other presents from aunts and uncles, most of whom lived in other parts of Canada.

Pete sat with these smaller presents – books, shirts, ties, socks, handkerchiefs, more books – piled around his feet. This was a happy time. He grinned at the sight of his mother and father, sitting close together on the couch, holding hands like a couple of kids, his father in a new smoking jacket, his mother with a new down-filled coat beside her.

"Gosh," he said. "Some bunch of stuff."

"How did you know I wanted new ski boots?" Sarah asked him.

"I saw your toes coming out through the old ones."

"If it wasn't impolite," she said, smiling at him, "I'd ask you where you ever managed to save up the money."

"I don't spend all my allowance every week, like some people I know," he said.

"Anyway," Sarah said, making a face at him, and turning to their parents, going over to hug each in turn, "it's sure a wonderful Christmas."

"All Christmases are wonderful," Pete said.

They all sat and beamed at each other.

"You'll have to get a steel cage built into your hockey gloves to protect that watch," Sarah said.

"Don't worry," said Pete, "this watch won't be playing any hockey with me. Fat holds the money and the watches." He paused, then went on. "Although I think I will wear it in one game, along with all the rest of my presents. I'd sure confuse the enemy, coming out there wearing a sweater and a wrist watch, and carrying a bunch of books!"

They laughed at him.

Sarah and Mrs. Gordon went to get breakfast. They'd all had fruit juice before opening their presents.

"Gee," Pete said to his dad, "there were times a month or so ago when I didn't figure I'd ever feel this way again so soon."

"Young people feel that way quite often before they get enough sense to know that every trouble passes eventually," his father said dryly. "But since you mention it, I was a little doubtful myself that you'd recover so fast."

Pete was restless. "Feels funny not to be out at the rink this morning," he said. "It's gotten to be a habit."

"I haven't had a chance lately to ask you. . . . How's Spunska coming along?"

"Good!" Pete was enthusiastic. "He powdered me one yesterday morning that shook my back teeth."

"You really play it that rough?"

Pete nodded. "Grouchy and I were rushing him. We got by him most of the time, of course. But this one time he feinted a check at Grouchy and then when Grouchy passed to me Spunska let me have it. A good play. . . . He's a funny guy. He always thinks he's going to hurt somebody. He does, too. But, I mean, you get over it. You know."

"Yes, I know."

Pete was wound up. He'd become so wrapped up in Spunska that he talked far more than usual when Spunska was the subject. "I get pretty excited about him," he said, subsiding. "I really believe he's going to be terrific."

A voice from the kitchen called, "Breakfast in five minutes!"

"You probably think I'm crazy," Pete said, "but I think Bill's going into a game this year."

"Should be all right to give him some experience now that you're out of the playoffs, anyway," his father said.

Pete lifted his head. "We're not really out of the playoffs, yet."

His dad burst out laughing. "My gosh, you've only tied one game out of four. Daniel Mac or Kelvin would have to lose just about all their next four games and you win all yours for you to catch one of them!"

Pete shrugged, but it wasn't a shrug of agreement that Northwest was out of it, no matter what the logic said.

"Breakfast!" Sarah called.

Pete rose, and his father put his hand on Pete's shoulder as he went by. "I still don't think you can make the playoffs."

Sarah caught the last few words. "Don't be a defeatist, Daddy! If it was Daniel Mac you'd be sure anything was possible."

Pete's dad laughed again. "Our son has two big projects now," he said to his wife. "One is to win the next four games for Northwest, and the other is to get Spunska into a game."

"I hope you get both your wishes, darling," she said.

"Me, too," said Sarah fervently.

"And me," said her father. "Ah, what a traitor I am to my alma mater."

After breakfast, Pete took a small parcel out from under the tree. It was addressed: *Merry Christmas to Bill, from Pete and Sarah*. Inside the elaborate wrapping was a roll of black tape, the kind used on hockey sticks, and a puck.

"Hey, Sarah," he said, "you coming with me over to Spunska's?"

"Soon as we've loaded the dishwasher," she called back. "Wait for me!"

They were quiet as they walked through the snowy streets. Others were walking, like them, carrying parcels, and today everyone smiled at everyone else. Pete's thoughts soon got back to hockey. Right now, Kelvin and Daniel Mac both were unbeaten. They'd tied 4-4 that night Northwest had tied Gordon Bell. Kelvin had three wins and a tie for seven points, Daniel two wins and two ties for six. Then came St. John's and Gordon Bell, each with a win and a tie for three points. and Finally, Northwest, one tie, one point.

He began humming the tune of "My Bonnie

Lies Over the Ocean." When Sarah heard it, she laughed and took his arm.

When they got to Spunska's they opened the door. "Merry Christmas!" they yelled.

There were more replies than there normally should have been, and when Bill and Mr. Spunska came into the hall to greet them a burly figure followed. It was Vic DeGruchy, with his frizzy hair slicked down and his big face shining like an apple and his suit showing signs of a very recent pressing, although it was rumpled now.

Apparently Christmas greetings had to be enthusiastic in Poland. Mr. Spunska kissed Sarah and shook hands with Pete. Bill shook hands with Pete and then grabbed Sarah and kissed her; Pete thought he'd never seen her prettier or happier as they stood together laughing and blushing until Grouchy said, "My turn, now."

He shook hands with Pete and with a courtly gesture made comical by his size and appearance, bowed low and kissed Sarah's hand.

They all trooped upstairs then to talk to Mrs. Spunska. She looked about the same, although her voice was a little stronger. She thanked Grouchy and Pete for helping Bill in the mornings. The way she did it almost made tears come to Pete's eyes. It did make the tears come to Sarah's. The Spunskas had put up their Christmas tree here in the bedroom, and for the next hour or two all of them sat there, crowding the room, eating nuts. Inevitably the talk got around to hockey and Pete noticed once a pleased look between the two elder Spunskas when, in the middle of a discussion, Bill put a handful of nuts on the bed coverlet and illustrated his idea of how a certain play might be made, and the others agreed.

CHAPTER 13

The Friday night after New Year's Gordon Bell had some unexpected rooters. The entire Northwest team sat up in the rafter seats and yelled and hooted and tried to urge Gordon Bell on to victory over Kelvin. Even Fat ran up from the dressing room every once in a while. It was Fat who had figured out the rather incredible possibility that if Kelvin got no better than a tie in its next four games, and Northwest won all its games, Northwest would finish ahead of Kelvin. He also figured that if Daniel Mac lost three out of its last four games they'd finish behind Northwest, if Northwest lost none. The funny thing was that nobody had laughed down in the sports office the noon Fat had produced this complicated set of possibilities. Rosy had called him Mr. Einstein for a while, but even that had passed.

So tonight Northwest rooted for Gordon Bell to beat Kelvin, but the rooting did no good. Kelvin's defence was weakened because of the absence of Barker, still out with his broken wrist, but the forward lines shot so straight and back-checked so hard that the deficiency wasn't noticeable. Kelvin was leading 6-0 in the second period when they got another bad break. Bush of Gordon Bell and Keenan of Kelvin went flying into a corner together after the puck and somehow Keenan fell. There was a groan of sympathy as his shoulder crashed into the boards and he convulsively flopped over on his back, groaning and holding his chest. Pete, on his feet, remembered his own injury and felt sorry for Keenan as they carried him off.

At the end of that second period it was time for the Northwest players to dress for their game with St. John's. When they got into the corridor they met two men of the St. John's Ambulance Corps carrying Keenan out to the hospital. Dr. Dartnell was hurrying to catch up.

When the young doctor saw Pete, he said, "You fellows seem determined that I'm not going to see a hockey game all the way through."

"What's the matter?" Pete asked.

"Broken collarbone."

Pete grimaced in sympathy. He had been hoping Keenan would be back in time for the game between Northwest and Kelvin next week. Pete had had nightmares about the way Keenan had outplayed him in the first game of the season and he wanted to show the people he could match Keenan, at least match him, when he was right. But now neither Keenan nor Barker would be playing.

It was Henry Bell who said it. "Well, I'm sorry to see anybody hurt. But I'd rather play Kelvin without Keenan and Barker than with them."

"You coward!" Rosy exclaimed, when he heard this. "It is not 'ow well you play the game, but 'oo you play against! Don't you know that?"

"Not in exactly those words," Bell said grinning.

"Never mind Kelvin," Red said from the end of the dressing room. "It's St. John's tonight."

Fat was over in the corner talking to Paterson, reeling off Northwest's mathematical playoff chances until the goalie looked dizzy. Grouchy was sitting in a corner alone. Pete went over and sat beside him.

"Bill sure looked good this morning, eh?"

"I was just thinking about him, too," Grouchy said. Spunska wasn't in the dressing room tonight. Upstairs there was an even bigger crowd than usual, a real scramble for seats, so he'd hung on to the one he had for the first game. The Kelvin and Gordon Bell players clumped along the corridor. Somebody poked his head in the door and called, "Kelvin 6, Gordon Bell 1. Game over."

"The trouble is," Grouchy went on, "where the heck would you put Bill on this team? He might be better than any of us when he really gets going, but in the meantime he'd make more mistakes than any of us and right now we can't afford mistakes."

"That's the understatement of the season," Pete said.

"If we either had won enough games that we could take a chance, or had lost enough that we didn't have a chance for the playoffs, we could let him play just for the experience. But we can't do that, yet."

"Yet?" Pete asked, grinning.

Grouchy smiled in return. "I mean we have to win a few more before we've got any points to give away."

Both smiled at the whimsy that they'd ever have points to give away. Red saw them, and felt good inside. He felt happy about the whole team now. If they could just keep away from injuries. That one to Gordon had set them on their ear once, just when they seemed to be getting started. Another one might be the killer, for this season. Out of all the hopeful kids who turned out as forwards to practices, there wasn't one he'd put on the ice even if he did have someone injured. He'd just have to go on with what he had, make them do double duty. That was only for forwards, of course. But he wasn't sure either about Spunska, for the defence. His own logic told him the kid couldn't be ready, although he did look a lot better in practices. But Red felt he couldn't afford to try him. Heck, the kid might blow sky-high. . . . Red's attention was diverted. Pete and Grouchy were laughing together in the corner now. Kids sure were funny! First they want to murder each other, and then they're bosom pals; and really, all along, both were good guys. But, St. John's tonight . . .

They were out in the corridor when the game officials and Lee Vincent came out of the room used by referees and linesmen.

Lee grabbed Red's arm above the elbow, held it in a friendly grip.

"I hate to rub this in," he said, "but didn't old Uncle Lee tell you that you were lucky to have Pete Gordon?"

"I'd hate to tell you how close you came to being wrong," Red said. "But I suppose newspapermen are wrong so often it wouldn't bother you anyway."

"Not a bit," Lee laughed. "It's the times we're right that we remember."

They were on the ice now, walking together toward the section in which the press box and players' bench were side by side.

"You really think you'll win a couple, Red?" Lee asked.

Red said, "We might win 'em all."

Lee stopped astonished on the ice and Red

hopped over the boards and gave the sportswriter a bland grin, thinking, Why'd I say that?

McMillan, the St. John's centre, faced Pete again in the opening face-off. McMillan was his old intent self. Pete stood with his legs wide apart, his stick pressed hard on the ice. As he saw the puck begin to drop he slapped at McMillan's stick and got his back fast enough to backhand a pass to Buchanan, and the game was on.

From the first, Paterson had a bad night. McMillan got a goal on a long shot from centre ice after only three minutes of the first period. But, even worse, a minute later a shot from the side bounded in off Paterson's leg. St. John's 2, Northwest 0.

Pete, whose line replaced Pincher Martin's on the ice after that second goal, went back to the goalie before the face-off.

"Don't let it bother you, Junior," he said. "We'll get them back."

"Gosh," Junior groaned. "I blew it! Should've had them both."

Rosy Duplessis came back and slapped him on the shoulder. "Bear down, boy!" he said. "Fat says we must win this one, or it throws out all his calculations. And think of how terrible that would be for all of us, having to listen to a whole new set of calculations!"

Paterson grinned, in spite of himself, slapped

his leg pads with the broad blade of his goal stick, and crouched. "Let's go! I'll smarten up!"

He did, too. As Red told him, in between periods, any goalie can have luck go against him for a while. But the goalie who can take the bad luck without getting jumpy and discouraged and letting in some by bad playing, he's the good goalie. "That kind can come back," Red said. "This team is going to get you some goals, and if you don't let in any more than the unlucky ones, you'll be doing all right."

But the second period started out badly, too. Pete's line was on, and he was having trouble with McMillan again. He tried every dodge he knew to shake the other boy, but without any results. But he kept his temper, remembering the other game, when Bell had lost his and got that disastrous penalty.

Apparently McMillan remembered it, too. One time, on the second or third line change of the period, he was fighting for the puck in a corner with Bell. From behind, Pete saw McMillan give Bell a stiff jolt in the ribs with the butt end of his stick. Bell, stung, jolted McMillan's ribs with his elbow. The only difference between the two rules infractions was that the referee saw Bell's elbow-smash, but didn't see McMillan's butt-end.

The referee skated in, blowing his whistle, touched Bell on the shoulder, and pointed to the penalty box.

Pete dashed in, raging.

"All right!" Bell said. "What about him!" He pointed to McMillan, who was skating away to his own bench.

"I could give you a misconduct for talking back," the referee said. "Neither of you is a captain or alternate!"

"Grouchy!" Pete yelled. "McMillan started it. He gave Hank a butt-end. I saw it."

DeGruchy towered over the referee. "How about it?" he said.

"I can't call what I don't see," the referee said, skating away. Pete, his lips compressed tightly, said, "All right, it won't do us any good to scream. Let's hold 'em now and murder 'em later."

The whistle blew. The puck dropped. Pete knocked down McMillan and was away into the St. John's zone. He outskated the defence and blasted a shot at the surprised goalie, who kicked it out with his skate. Coming around behind the net he saw McMillan bracing himself to check and Pete braced himself, too, and McMillan went down again, although Pete was shaken. Pete had the puck again. St. John's had the edge in manpower, but they couldn't get the puck from Pete. He passed out to the blueline to Rosy Duplessis, stretched to try to get a return pass that was too far ahead of him, went into the corner, dodged out of the way as a St. John's defenceman lunged at him, and was dragging the puck out of the corner one-handed when McMillan, up again, slashed at him with his stick in an attempt to make him lose the puck.

From the corner of his eye he saw the referee's hand go into the air, the signal for a deferred penalty. He knew it must be against McMillan. The referee wouldn't blow his whistle until a St. John's player had the puck, so that the calling of the penalty against St. John's wouldn't also end the threat to the St. John's net. Paterson raced to get off the ice and let another forward on – Pincher Martin. The Northwest goal was empty but that was safe because as soon as Northwest lost the puck the penalty whistle would be blown. As it happened, Pincher didn't quite make it into the play at all. Pete passed back to Rosy, who drove a shot on goal. Pete was on the rebound like a flash. The goalie didn't have a chance. Northwest was back in the game, even though still trailing 2-1 and still one man short.

Pete ragged the puck after the face-off for thirty seconds until Bell was back on the ice. Then Red sent out the Hurry Berton line with Rosy and Jamieson.

"Boy, I'd like to be out there," Grouchy said to Pete on the bench.

"Can't play all the time, you lunkhead," Pete said.

It slipped out, the word *lunkhead*. As soon as he said it he was sorry, because you have to be awfully good friends to start calling a guy names. Especially Grouchy, with his quick temper. But Grouchy just grinned.

And the goal had fired up the Northwests. The five of them simply skated into the St. John's zone and passed the puck around as if they had it on strings. When the Chief finally blasted it home from ten feet in front to tie the score, in the press box Lee Vincent had to laugh aloud. "I counted nine passes before that goal!"

Not only that, but the next one came faster – Rosy's first goal of the season. The crowd bellowed, first with the natural reaction to the goal, and then to the antics of Rosy. He jumped into the air and tried to clap his feet together like an acrobat, failed, fell, got up again, and his long war whoop could be heard even above all the other cheering. Three-two for Northwest.

The Northwest players mobbed Rosy, Pete among them, laughing, while the referee stood at centre ice and impatiently tooted on his whistle.

After the commotion died down, Pete and

McMillan were facing one another again. Pete spoke again. "Cost your club the lead, McMillan," Pete needled. "Feel good?"

"Shut up, Gordon," the referee said.

McMillan said nothing. He apparently wasn't going to get drawn into a feud with Pete again. This was the second night he'd tried to get Pete riled into a penalty and now he gave up. He still checked hard, but he played a hard-driving clean game and a few minutes later started the play for the tying goal. He shot at the goal, but Pete deflected the puck as it left McMillan's stick. The puck unluckily went straight to the stick of another St. John's player. Paterson was way out of position, didn't see the puck until he was picking it out of the net.

But then Pincher Martin took the game in hand. He had a flair for the spectacular and he used it now. On the face-off after the tying goal he got the draw from the St. John's centre and stickhandled away from his man down centre ice. A defenceman lunged. Martin stepped around him. The defenceman sprawled on the ice. The centre, Martin's check, came dashing in fast. Martin stopped dead and the other centre went on by, trying to turn. Then the other defenceman had his go. Martin poked the puck between his legs, changed pace like a flash, shifted around the flailing defenceman, and was in the clear in front of the net. With the whole St. John's team, suddenly snapped out of their sleepwalking, barging toward him, Martin picked a hole and slapped the puck into it and Northwest was ahead again, and Pete, looking at the St. John's bench, saw the St. John's coach take off his hat, crumple it into a ball, wind up and hurl it to the floor.

The next goal, thirty-two seconds later, was as fast as the last one had been slow, like a jitterbug number coming after a minuet. From the centre face-off Martin slapped the puck over to Benny Wong, who took it in full stride, lost it, but followed the puck carrier around behind the Northwest net, fighting all the way. Winston Kryschuk came in from the other wing and got it. The pale, wispy little guy stickhandled over the blueline, gathering speed, saw Wong moving fast at the other blueline, and passed. Wong swept around the defence and passed across the goalmouth to Martin who feinted a shot and passed back to Wong and the chunky Chinese boy banged it into the net. Northwest 5. St. John's 3. And bedlam.

In the third period Northwest played it straight and cosy. Red told them, between periods, not to hold back if they saw a break, but to wait for the breaks before they took chances. No breaks came, so they took no chances. St. John's got one more goal on a last-minute wild scramble in front of Paterson. The game ended Northwest 5, St. John's 4.

Red had wondered, after the tie with Gordon Bell, what would happen if they ever won one. Now he found out. It was odd, but the big crowd, after one big bellow, was quieter than usual, sensing the deep feeling in the way the Northwest players were pummelling each other. Everybody but Paterson. Pete skated over to him.

"What the heck's the matter, Junior?" Pete asked. "You hurt, or something?"

"Four goals on me," Paterson groaned. "Gosh, I might have lost us the game!"

"You dope! Come on! We won it! Sometime when we get only one goal you just won't be able to let any in. But we got five tonight. Four against us didn't hurt a bit!"

In the final puffed-out cessation of the noise a few minutes later Fat could be heard in the corner explaining the situation to Lee Vincent, who had come down with the Northwesters. "Now, Mr. Vincent," Fat was saying excitedly, "according to my calculations . . ."

That was as far as he got before the laughter drowned him out. He returned to his work, trying to look mad because they wouldn't let him talk, but nothing could hide the look in his eyes. His heroes finally had won a game.

CHAPTER 14

Pete and Bill lingered one noon over their hot chocolate in the Northwest cafeteria. They were talking about a play they had practised that morning, Bill breaking fast in end-to-end dashes. Bill was quieter than usual.

"How's your mother?" Pete asked.

"A little better. But it's so slow." He paused, then said in a rush, "I wish I were good enough to get into a game! I have a feeling it would help."

"I wish you could get in, too," Pete said quietly. "I think you're ready."

Bill's face brightened. "Do you?"

"I sure do."

"But the coach wouldn't change now, when we're going well," Bill said reluctantly. "It wouldn't be a good idea."

A few minutes later, Pete rose to leave. Bill decided he was going to have another piece of pie.

Pete walked through the halls. Nothing anybody could do. Bill was ready, if there was a defence injury. He might not be as steady as the others to start. But he'd be good. Gosh, when the crowds got a load of that mad dash of his down centre ice . . .

But it would probably be next year, now. He put the matter out of his mind.

He stopped by one of the wide windows in the upper hall and looked out at the snow. It was a real prairie blizzard, and he was glad he was inside. The wind was from the north, driving snow before it so hard that it was almost impossible to see the row of houses across from the school. A boy and girl stopped beside him. He didn't know their names, but everybody in Northwest stopped to speak to Pete Gordon now, or any other member of the hockey team. Funny. As he walked on, later, it occurred to him that the feeling here about the hockey team was even greater than it had been at Daniel Mac. Why? Maybe because the school was so new. Maybe the rest of the kids, in a way, had felt the same way he had at first, that this place was empty, too new. Now they had something to hold on to. The hockey team was unbeaten in its last two starts, and the game with Kelvin was coming up this Friday.

Pete nodded and spoke to many others as he went slowly down the stairs. At the sports office, he tapped on the door, opened it a little, and looked in.

"Come on in," Red said. "There's nobody here but us sardines."

The office *was* crowded. Fat was sitting by the window stitching a tear in a pair of hockey pants. Red was at his desk, with the morning paper open at the sports pages in front of him. Grouchy, Junior Paterson, Rosy Duplessis and Gordon Jamieson sat on straight chairs around the wall; Benny Wong and Winston Kryschuk on the floor.

Everybody grinned or waved a hand, greeting Pete.

Red chuckled. "Every time I look at the league standings it makes me laugh. We had so many goals scored on us the first few games that we'll sure not win any trophies for defensive work, anyway."

"I'm just a human sieve in there," Paterson said morosely.

"Junior!" Rosy said. "If you don't stop that crying we will start calling you something. You are always moaning and groaning. Inspector Heartburn, you! Do you 'ear me moan when a man gets by me? No! No use to worry, I tell you. You will get an ulcer."

Pete walked back behind Red and glanced at the league standings, which were printed along with a story about the high school hockey double-header tomorrow night, Northwest vs. Kelvin and Daniel Mac vs. St. John's Tech.

175

Here's how the standings looked:

High School Hockey League

TEAM	PLAYED	WON	LOST	TIED	GOALS FOR	GOALS AGAINST	POINTS
Kelvin	5	4	0	1	29	14	9
Daniel Mac	4	2	0	2	18	9	6
St. John's	5	1	3	1	16	16	3
Northwest	5	1	3	1	12	24	3
Gordon Bell	5	1	3	1	8	20	3

"Lee Vincent gives us a pretty fair chance against Kelvin, in his column," Red said. "But don't get overconfident."

"No!" Rosy said. "It would not do to let overconfidence cause us to lose our grip on our tie for last place!"

Red laughed with the others. "I'm serious," he said. "Kelvin's a tough hockey club, even with Keenan and Barker out. They've got boys there who could almost step into minor pro hockey right now."

"But Keenan and Barker being out sort of hacks them down to our size, I think," drawled Gordon Jamieson.

"Maybe you're right," Red said. "I'll tell you one thing. If you can beat Kelvin, I'll figure our season has been a success even if we don't win another game."

The blizzard, which was still blowing the next night, didn't lessen the crowd much, but indirectly it hurt the Northwest team. Pincher Martin, who lived about twenty blocks from the school in a bungalow which was almost out on the bald prairie, had a frostbitten foot from the night before.

He had been at Spunska's. Since the word got around about Mrs. Spunska being sick, and the way it lifted her spirits to see that Bill had many friends, many of the players had taken to dropping in there in the evenings. When Martin left, the night before the game, Mrs. Spunska was asleep. He'd forgotten his overshoes, and he didn't like to go back and ring the doorbell and maybe wake her up. And Bill had been headed up for bed when he left. So he didn't go back. In his long walk home through the zero weather and blowing snow, the cold easily got through his running shoes. Now his foot was paining him greatly.

Pete never had felt anything quite like the atmosphere in the Northwest dressing room before this Kelvin game. The place was quiet. All the boisterousness was gone. Pete recognized the strain. It was funny, when the club had nothing but forlorn hopes, everybody had laughed and talked before the game. Now that the hopes weren't quite so forlorn, although they still were forlorn enough, they all acted as if they were playing for the Stanley Cup.

Half a dozen of them bawled Pincher Martin

out for not going back for his overshoes. They yammered away at him until finally he protested. "Holy cow! You guys! I get nagged enough at home and at school!" He was half laughing now. "Leave me one place where I can be a dope and get away with it!"

They subsided a little.

"I won't let the team down," Pincher said. "I can skate all right."

But Pete, sitting next to him on the bench, saw him wince as he pulled on his skate boot. He saw also that when Martin tightened the laces, his left foot was much looser than the other. He saw Martin notice it, too, and with a set face the boy tried to tighten the left boot. The pain must have been great, because despite the resolve on his face he immediately loosened it again. When Martin stood up, Pete thought the left boot looked wobbly.

"Can't get the darn thing tight," Martin said in a low voice, exasperated. "Hurts too much. Maybe when I get going on it . . ."

But the first time he was on the ice it was quite plain that he couldn't play his usual game that night. Every step was pain. After a few minutes of the hard-checking, tight first period, Red benched him and moved Duplessis up to centre the Martin line, which left Northwest with only three defencemen, DeGruchy, Jamieson and Lawrence.

Red stood behind his players' bench and stared grimly out at the boy Kelvin had brought up from the scrubs to replace Barker. Heck! The kid up from Kelvin's scrubs was almost as good as Barker! Actually, Red thought, he was better than any defenceman Northwest had, except DeGruchy.

And yet, look at my guys go! They don't back down an inch. The Kelvin kid may be good, but when he knocks 'em down they keep on getting up. Chief Big Canoe got in for a hard shot on the Kelvin goal. Kelvin had been outplaying Northwest for ten minutes but that was the hardest test on goal of the period. Red shook his head. He couldn't quite understand this hockey team of his.

As if to remind him why Northwest could make it tough for any of them, Grouchy chose that minute for one of his sensational rushes. This time he got the puck behind his own net. The Kelvin centre tried to stop the rush before it started, cutting in fast for a sweeping poke check. DeGruchy eluded the check without changing stride and then he was picking up speed, Benny Wong with him, stride for stride, ready for a pass. Grouchy hit the Kelvin defence, passing at the last instant to Wong. Bodies flew in all directions as the two defencemen sandwiched Grouchy and all three went down, while Wong sped in to the front of the goal, stopped dead in a shower of flying ice scrapings to let his check go speeding past him, then passed across the goal crease to Kryschuk, who tipped the puck easily into the side of the net.

The Northwest team was electrified. Okay, we're leading. Let's get some more. The next time Pete was on the ice he skated rings around the opposition centre, fed pass after pass to his wings, and it was just a matter of time. Bell got the second goal on a pass from Pete, and Buchanan got the third after a neat passing play between Bell and DeGruchy and Pete. They trooped down the stairs to the dressing room after the first period, holding at 3-0 lead over the league's leading team, a team never before beaten this season.

"We don't even need you, Pincher!" Rosy yelped.

Pincher grinned painfully.

Red wished he felt as confident as Rosy. This was like a dream, this 3-0 lead. But he looked at Grouchy, stretched out on the bench. Grouchy had played most of the first period and was tired. And that was bad.

Red was following a system of alternating Jamieson and Lawrence on the defence with DeGruchy. The one time he'd put Lawrence and Jamieson on defence together, Paterson had been forced to make three terrific saves to prevent a Kelvin score. Red wondered if he should move either Lawrence or Jamieson up to Martin's place and drop Duplessis back. Rosy was just a shade better as a defenceman than the other two. But it would be taking from one pocket to fill another. Duplessis was the only one of the three fast enough to centre Wong and Kryschuk. Darn it, he sure needed reserves. The idea of dressing Spunska crossed his mind, but it was too late. If Martin had only admitted that his foot was that bad . . .

Before the second period started, he said, "We'll try her the same way this period. For a while, anyway."

Before his eyes, in the next few minutes, the Northwest team began to fade. They were trying hard, but Kelvin's coach, a cagey old-timer named Tommy Watson, saw the fix Red was in and took advantage of it. He poured Kelvin reserves over the boards. Their orders apparently were to skate, skate, skate, wear 'em down, make 'em skate with you, and when you're puffed out come back and we'll replace you. And it worked. The Northwest team obviously was wilting. The Northwest cheerleaders saw it and were doubly active, and the Kelvin section, stunned by the first period, began to take heart again, seeing the tide of battle slowly swing against Northwest.

Then Red made his decision. He hoped it wasn't too late.

"Martin," he said, "can you skate at all?"

"Sure, Coach," Martin said eagerly. "Not my best, but I can skate."

"Take your line out at the next whistle."

Red sent Duplessis back to defence and brought Grouchy off. He practically had to hold Grouchy down, but he had him on the bench for four minutes, while the Northwesters held desperately to their lead. Then Red put his defence combinations back in shape again, Grouchy with Jamieson, Duplessis with Lawrence. And the thing he had counted on took place. When Martin was on the ice the rest of the team was so conscious of his limp, his lack of speed, and the constant look of pain on his face that they checked as if they'd be burned at the stake if they allowed the puck across the Northwest blueline.

Red slowly began to relax. The line was holding. For a few minutes, it had looked bad. He asked each time Martin came in, "How's the foot? Can you feel it?" He knew that as long as there was circulation there was nothing to fear. And Martin always said he could feel it, sure. He wished sometimes he couldn't, it hurt so much. It was like one big chilblain, but he could feel it all right.

Ironically, just when it seemed that Northwest was going to get all the breaks in the game, Kelvin got one. Stimers, the Kelvin winger, momentarily outfought Bell for the puck in a corner, spotted the other forward, Josephson, a step or two clear of Buchanan at the other side of the rink, and tried a long desperate pass just as Bell knocked him down. If the pass had got through to Josephson, it would have been no good to Kelvin anyway, because Buchanan saw it coming and tied up Josephson. But in midflight the puck struck a skate and deflected past Paterson into a corner of the goal.

Paterson, who had been fighting like a tiger against the team that had kept him on the bench all last year as sub goalie, swung his goal stick above his head like a club and crashed it down on the ice. "Gol darn it!" he shouted. "And I was going to get a shutout!"

Pete tried to calm him. So did DeGruchy. Paterson wouldn't be calmed. And maybe it was just as well. Kelvin, fired by this lucky break, stormed around the net for the next two or three minutes and fired shot after shot at the goal only to be met with Paterson's angry imitation of a whirling dervish. He never stopped yelling his rage, and he did the splits, and kicked out shots, caught them with his hands, batted them away with his stick. Once he even dashed out of his net to beat Stimers to a puck. He held them out. The second period ended without a further score. Northwest 3, Kelvin 1.

And somehow, skating until each boy felt he could skate no more, checking, covering up for

Martin, knocking the man down if they couldn't get him any other way, Northwest hung out through the third period.

The crowd, caught up by the spirit of this tired, staggering team which was trying to accomplish the upset of the season, cheered in a rising roar that reached a crescendo in the last minute of play when Kelvin finally took its goalie from the ice and sent six forwards to the attack. All to gain, nothing to lose; and on the first play, with each Northwester checking one man there was still one left uncovered for a hot shot that Paterson couldn't handle, to cut the margin to 3-2.

He was silent now, dogged, intent. They blasted shot after shot at him. Grouchy knocked down two men at a time. Pete flew from one man to another spoiling shots, knocking them down, springing at boys who outweighed him twenty pounds. And the minute seemed like a year.

Lee Vincent sat in the press box with his fingers so tight on his pencil that his hand hurt. At the bench, Red put his hands on Pincher Martin's shoulders and pulled him this way and that, making every check. Fat was gulping, his lips quivering, yelling, silent, his face red as fire and then white. Up in the stands Bill Spunska held Sarah's hand and jerked this way and that with another desperate body check by Grouchy, another miraculous save by Paterson, another dashing attempt by Pete to get the puck out of there. Pete's dad shouted, his mother almost cried. They were on their feet now, everybody, yelling, watching in a torrent of noise the rounded rectangle of ice where twelve boys fought as if for their lives, fought on even after the buzzer had gone to end the game, because there was so much noise that nobody heard the buzzer.

CHAPTER 15

It was two weeks later. About five p.m. Pete was eating an early dinner, reading Lee Vincent's column in the *Telegram*:

> Four games left in the high school hockey league, two tonight and two next Friday, and the second playoff spot is still wide open. Before the season started Daniel Mac and Kelvin looked like sure bets for the two playoff places. I wouldn't have taken fifty to one, even in doughnuts instead of dollars, that Northwest would have a chance. And now look at them. It's one time when I'm not unhappy to be wrong.
>
> A lot of people have been trying to figure out what makes Northwest tick. They started the season as an unknown bunch of scrubs, except for Pete Gordon. But the most effective defenceman in the league now is Vic DeGruchy - not too stylish, but he doesn't need style.
>
> Gordon is still the best centre in the league, despite hot competition from gents like Keenan of Kelvin and McMillan of St. John's. The funny thing is that the rest of the Northwest team has turned out to be very strong as a unit, although only two or

three of the players stand out individually. Right now they've got a chance to make the playoffs, which would be an astonishing achievement for a team playing its first year in the league.

I say a chance. It depends on many things. St. John's Tech helped a couple of weeks ago, after Northwest had beaten Kelvin, when they upset Daniel Mac 3-2. Then last week, when Northwest didn't play, Daniel Mac took Gordon Bell 5-2, about as expected, and Kelvin - with Barker back, his wrist still taped heavily - tied St. John's 6-6.

That left the standings where they are today, with Kelvin in first place with ten points, Daniel Mac second with eight, St. John's third with six, Northwest fourth with five, and Gordon Bell, the league's in-and-out team, last with three points.

You might think that Northwest's chances shouldn't be as good as St. John's but Northwest has two games left, St. John's only one. Therefore, Northwest's potential is another four points, to total nine; St. John's potential is another two points, or eight.

Daniel Mac's potential is another four points, too, but it isn't as strong a potential as the others. Daniel has to play Kelvin tonight. With Keenan and Barker back, the Kelvins will be at full strength, and therefore should win. And then Daniel has to play Northwest next Friday, and right now nobody in the league likes playing Northwest, because apparently these ignorant Northwesters never read the paper and don't know that they're supposed to roll over and play dead.

> Anyway, we'll know better tonight. Northwest's hopes would vanish entirely if they happened to lose to Gordon Bell. And Daniel would cinch a playoff spot by beating Kelvin. But neither of those possibilities is likely. I think you'll see the league knotted tighter than ever after tonight's play.

Pete finished his steak and the column about the same time, picked out an apple for his dessert, then put on his coat and walked down to Spunska's house. His parents and Sarah were going to drive to the game later in the car, but Pete hadn't seen Mrs. Spunska since Tuesday.

Bill answered the door.

"Hi," Pete said, reaching in for the broom to sweep the snow from his overshoes. "Thought I'd come early so we could go down together. How's your mother?"

"About the same. But the doctor was here today."

"What did he say?"

Mr. Spunska had come into the hall, carrying his newspaper, and Bill glanced at him. "He was interested to hear about the boys coming to see her," Mr. Spunska said. "He said that was the best thing that could have happened to her, showing her how much you boys regard our son."

Pete was embarrassed and so was Bill. But of course Pete felt good to hear it.

They asked Pete to eat with them, but he explained that he had eaten. When they were eating, he went upstairs quietly. Mrs. Spunska's bedroom door was open. She looked some better, younger, with the soft light of her bed lamp behind her. She motioned to him to come in and spoke in her low voice. "Peter, I'm glad to see you again. . . . It is nice of you to come. . . . How are you?"

"Fine. How are you?"

"I just have no energy." She paused. "I hope it will not be too long. Sarah was here today. She has been here almost every day. . . ." She smiled as if they shared a private joke. "She and Bill, they are like brother and sister."

Pete grinned. "Not quite," he said.

She smiled. "That is right. Not quite."

"Could I get you anything?" Pete asked.

"Nothing . . . Peter, how is Bill progressing?"

"Fine. He could play for us now, if there was an opening on the team. Now that we're winning, though, the coach won't change it. But next year, he'll be one of the best . . ."

"You're not just saying that to make me feel better?"

Pete was definite, and surprised, too. "I sure am not!"

Her head turned on the pillow toward him, and Pete had a strange feeling. In that light, he could see her as a girl, before the lines of worry had come. It must be bad to have to put one whole life behind you, and build another.

"I'm glad," she said in a low voice. "You know, it is not the game, so much, with me . . . I have never been interested in games before. But since Bill became so interested in hockey, I have read some about it, too. In the professional leagues there are so many names . . . Gretzky, Hawerchuk, Stastny. Those are names from our part of Europe and our neighbours. I know that usually a family must live in a country one generation, or sometimes two or three, before the children are accepted for everything. But it seems to me that sport is different. It is what you are, not what you have been or what your parents have been. . . ."

Her words made a lump in his throat. He'd never thought of it just that way before, but it was true.

"You won't say any of this to Bill?" she asked anxiously. "I mean, I do not wish such a thing to become another pressure on him, a feeling that he must succeed in sport. It is just that I can see that if he does succeed it will be easier for him, everything will be so much easier quickly. . . . I am silly. This is a woman's anxiety. I wanted to tell someone. I told you. . . ."

"I won't say anything," Pete said. He rose,

hearing Bill coming up the stairs. "Time to go now, I guess."

"Good luck," she said, smiling.

CHAPTER 16

It was strange, after that talk, what happened in the game against Gordon Bell that night.

When Spunska left the dressing room, rather sadly, to find a seat, he had some trouble, the rink was so full. Northwest got to the ice first, and was well warmed up even before Gordon Bell showed. Some of the Gordon Bell players looked mad, and others were subdued. There was an odd feeling to the half-lackadaisical, half-angry way they went through their warm-up.

"That coach of theirs chewed their ears off," DeGruchy said, coming up beside Pete. "One of the guys, that little centre, Bush, he knows Duplessis. Told him that."

"Something's sure the matter, anyway," Pete said.

Gordon Bell's coach was a former professional hockey player, Biff McCarty. He'd been known in the big leagues as a very tough operator who never quit. Pete thought that a guy with that kind of temperament probably took it pretty hard when a team he coached let him down like this, and yet possibly another kind of coach would have gotten more out of the players. . . . A sort of vicious circle. Certainly when they were right, like the night they beat St. John's and the night they tied Northwest, they were hard to beat.

Grouchy took a shot on Paterson and came back out to Pete.

"Bush was telling Rosy that the coach really gave that big Forsyth the works. He told Forsyth that before he'd be any good as a hockey player he had to get it into his head that he had to play just as hard when he was ten goals down as he did when he was ten goals up. As much as said Forsyth quit when they got behind."

Pete, skating back a minute later from a practice shot, saw Forsyth slam the puck angrily into the boards after missing a shot. Too bad. Forsyth was a real hot hockey player, plenty of natural ability. He felt a little sorry for Forsyth, remembering another hot hockey player, named Pete Gordon, who once had looked to some people as if he didn't try too hard.

But it turned out he needn't have felt sorry for Forsyth. The boy had his own way of working out his bad temper, and it just about ruined the game.

From the opening face-off, Pete got the puck, drove in on defence and Forsyth knocked him down. He didn't mind that. He got up, and was skating around Forsyth when he heard, "That's not the last time you'll be flat on your pants, tonight, shorty."

Pete didn't even look back at him. He was chasing his check, Bush, keeping close. A pass came toward Bush. Pete tipped it over to Duplessis. Rosy was away like a shot down centre ice. Pete and Bell and Buchanan couldn't get back in time to take the pass so Rosy went in alone, shifted past the defencemen, and blasted a shot past the goalkeeper just as Forsyth, charging back to cover up for his defencemate's error, dealt him a terrific blow from behind and knocked him skidding into the boards. Rosy was up like a flash, dropping his stick and his gloves. Henry Bell grabbed him just as he was about to tear into Forsyth.

Pete came up just in time to hear Forsyth say, "Come on, you big Frog, if you wanta fight I'm ready."

The referee got there, then, and thumbed Forsyth off for charging. Pete helped Rosy pick up his gloves and stick.

"That guy's going to make some trouble," he said.

"For himself, mostly," Rosy said. "Boy, I am glad Bell grabbed me. I was going to murder him. I probably would have got myself into the penalty box."

"Don't feel right for me to be a peacemaker," Bell grinned, and the others grinned with him, remembering his feuds with McMillan of St. John's.

The rest of the short-handed Gordon Bells dug in after the face-off to keep the score from going higher. When Forsyth came back to the ice the Northwesters were peppering the Gordon Bell goal but couldn't get it in. The penalty seemed to have cooled him off a bit – for a few minutes, anyway.

On the bench, while play went on, Pete told Red what Forsyth had said to Rosy, calling him a big Frog. Red felt an immediate pang of apprehension. He had many different nationalities on his team, and he was proud of it. It made him white-hot when he heard of this kind of talk.

"If there's any more of it, tell me," he said to Pete. "I'll put a stop to that, if I have to go to the Gordon Bell principal."

"It doesn't bother me," Rosy said.

"It might bother some of the others." Red watched Benny Wong out there, skating his heart out. On the bench in front of him sat Big Canoe, the Indian boy the others called the Chief. And yet Red wasn't worried about the Chief. He was a well-adjusted kid and could look after himself. He wasn't so worried about Duplessis, either. But Wong, he was a quiet kid, wouldn't say boo to a goose. . . .

All were Canadians and didn't need any derogatory racial tags.

For a while through the first period and part of the second, Red managed to keep Benny on the bench while Forsyth was on the Gordon Bell defence. But one time, midway in the second, he couldn't get him off fast enough.

The players on the ice then for Northwest were Jamieson, DeGruchy, Martin – whose foot bothered him no longer – Kryschuk and Wong. A Gordon Bell rush was broken up by Jamieson, who passed up to Benny Wong at the red line. Wong was all alone for the instant, and instead of waiting for his line to catch up he broke in fast on the Gordon Bell defence. He cut in to centre and the two defencemen came together to check him, and then suddenly Wong cut to the left and Forsyth followed him. He seemed sure to skate Wong off into the corner when suddenly Wong pulled a trick he had gotten down to perfection. Just as Forsyth tensed himself for a ferocious check that would have sent Benny flying into the boards, the little Northwester stopped in his tracks and Forsyth, unable to regain his balance, hurtled by and hit the boards himself with a crash while Benny sped into centre and blasted a rising shot into a corner of the net. The crowd booed Forsyth. Hockey fans, like most people, like to see a little guy get the better of a big one, and there was a lot of laughter mixed with the booing, and then there was a big cheer for Benny as he skated back up the ice. Forsyth got up and skated slowly to his defence position, glaring at Benny. Pete noticed it. Heck, the guy looked as if Benny had pulled a dirty trick on him, when really he'd just made an excellent play.

Red hesitated. The Martin line was going so well he left them on. But on the next play after the face-off Wong and Forsyth tangled in the corner, along with Jamieson, all three fighting for the puck. When Red saw Benny suddenly stiffen and look at Forsyth, and Jamieson for an instant look as if he was going to hit Forsyth, he knew instinctively what had happened again.

He sent the Berton line over the boards, and when Benny sat before him he leaned over and said in the boy's ear, "That big ape bothering you?"

"A little," Benny said, after a pause.

"Calling you names?"

"He said I was a yellow Chink."

Red walked to the gate to the ice and yelled to the referee. The official waved him away. Red waited until a face-off and then called

DeGruchy over and told him to tell the referee he wanted to see him, something important. The referee came over. Red told him what had happened.

The referee said, "If I hear him do it, I'll give him a game misconduct. I can't do anything until I hear him."

"I'll protest to the school board if you don't stop it."

"Look," the referee said, "suppose the Gordon Bell coach complained about one of your guys and I had no evidence to support it. Wouldn't you scream if I put your guy off with no evidence except from the team he's playing against? But I'll watch."

Red chewed his nails through the rest of the second period, but the matter didn't come to a head until the third.

In the first two minutes of the final period Wong scored Northwest's third goal, on a screened shot from the blueline, while Forsyth was plunging toward him. And Pete saw Forsyth say something more to Benny, and Jamieson turned and spoke sharply to Forsyth, who ignored him.

The referee dashed in and spoke to Wong, and Wong just skated away. Red was yelling from the players' bench, but the referee was getting rattled. He was trying to track this down, but he couldn't stay next to Forsyth all night and let the play go on unwatched elsewhere.

"What did he say?" Pete asked Jamieson a minute later.

Jamieson didn't answer directly. "The dirty loudmouth," he said slowly.

"Take it easy," Pete warned. "We don't want to toss this game away by getting penalties."

But Forsyth, who had gotten away with it so far, got worse as the game went on. Red was torn. He wanted to appeal directly to someone in authority who would either tell the boy to shut up, or remove him from the ice. But to do that he'd have to leave the bench, and he didn't want to leave the bench. They had this game sewed up, if they could hold. And they could hold, if Forsyth didn't goad them into blowing it. A thing like this made him feel sick to his stomach, but he couldn't be in two places at once.

He could feel his players slowly reaching a pitch of fever. Red was glad Jamieson had been near Wong when all this happened, not Rosy, or DeGruchy. Those hotheads would have torn into Forsyth and the resulting penalty might have cost Northwest the game. But Jamieson was one of the mildest boys on the team, stood first in his class, and hadn't had a penalty all season. Red felt sure he could hold his temper.

The minutes ticked off slowly, two minutes to

play, one, thirty seconds, ten and then the buzzer sounded to end the game. Northwest had won, 3-0.

Simultaneously with the buzzer, Jamieson took off from his defence spot towards Forsyth. He dropped his stick at his own blueline and his gloves at centre ice and Forsyth saw him coming just in time to get his own hands up. Then Jamieson was on him. The force of his rush knocked Forsyth to the ice and Jamieson was on top of him and had him by the shoulders and was hammering away wildly with his fists. Forsyth rolled and knocked Jamieson off and got to his feet as the other players and game officials dashed in to hold them. But they couldn't hold Jamieson. Like many mild boys, when he did lose his temper it was gone for keeps. He suddenly broke free, knocked a few people away from Forsyth, and slugged it out with him again.

This time DeGruchy, on the outside of the group of players, didn't help pull either of the fighters away. Jamieson was doing much better than holding his own, so when the next rush of players came to separate them, DeGruchy pushed them back. "The first guy who touches them gets me to fight," he said.

The referee made a dash to get in there, but got enveloped in the crowd, now swarming to the ice. The rink police tried to get the fans back to their seats. The fight went on. When the police finally got around to the pugilists, Forsyth was in a corner with his elbows up guarding his face, and Jamieson was sobbing, hands at his side, daring Forsyth to come out and fight. The bigger boy didn't respond. Just before the police got there, Jamieson turned away of his own accord and led the Northwest team to the dressing room.

Red stood outside until every player was in, then went in and locked the door, and the angry chatter suddenly was stilled. Benny Wong was unlacing his skates, Jamieson was sitting in a corner with his head in his hands. The others, Pete and Grouchy and all the rest, sat and waited for what Red had to say.

The coach said it slowly. "The kid had it coming," he said. "I'm not going to say this was the best thing to do, though. I was going to protest to the league council right after the game. But maybe this was better, at that. . . . There'll be no evading the issue, now." He went over and touched Jamieson's shoulder. "Thanks for waiting until the game was over."

"Hey!" Paterson exclaimed. "Paterson got a shutout!"

That broke the tension temporarily, as they congratulated him. But Jamieson got up suddenly and went into the washroom back of the showers and was sick. And just then there was a knock on the door.

Red opened it to the referee, Dick Dunsford.

"Red," he said, "can you come with me a minute."

"I hope you believe me now," Red said.

"I believe you," Dunsford said sadly.

Red walked down the hall to the referee's room. Lee Vincent was there, sitting on a bench; Biff McCarty, Gordon Bell coach; the game officials; Mr. Anderson, the Northwest principal, a spare youngish man; and Mr. Donnelly from Gordon Bell, grey-haired, with a worried look on his plump, lined face.

"Do you want some of my kids to come in here and tell what Forsyth called our kid Wong all through the game?" Red demanded immediately.

"That's not necessary, Red," said Mr. Anderson. "Mr. McCarty here has told me that some of his boys came to him and told him the same thing. The boys on his team were just as disgusted as yours."

"Why didn't you do something about it, then?" Red asked McCarty.

"I didn't know until after the game." McCarty's big tough face was angry and concerned.

"But," Mr. Anderson said, "no matter how

much provocation there was, we can't have questions like that settled with fist fights. That's what we have a league council for. Next week, when everybody has had a chance to cool off a little, we'll have an inquiry."

"That's all you want me for?" Red asked curtly.

"Yes," Mr. Anderson said.

Red turned and left the room. Inquiry. He knew what that would mean. Suspensions. There should be one suspension, all right. But Red was afraid there would be two.

McCarty followed him. "Sorry, boy," he said to Red. "I wish I'd known in time to stop it."

Red managed to muster a smile. "Wouldn't like to go back to school, would you? At Northwest? We could sure use an experienced defenceman."

When he was opening the dressing room door to go back and tell the boys what had happened, he thought fleetingly of Bill Spunska, wondered if he really was ready.

CHAPTER 17

Pete had never gone through a week like it. Every morning, his first thought was, Will that darn inquiry be today? Red had told him what the principals had said, that they'd hold it several days later to give the boys involved a chance to calm down, a chance to sweat over what they had done, but Pete didn't think they'd also meant that every boy on the Northwest team and dozens besides in the school would have to sweat it out, too. And yet that was what was happening.

He was in the history class on Thursday morning when there was a knock on the door. The boy nearest it answered.

He turned. "Gord Jamieson and Pete Gordon. You're wanted at the principal's office."

There was a murmur through the class. Everyone knew what this meant. Even Mr. Ross, the history teacher. He said, "Good luck, boys. Come back alive."

Pete and Jamieson walked into the hall. The

principal's office was on the next floor down. They walked along together, silently. Nothing to say, Pete thought. We've both gone through this week. What a week! He knew it must have been worse for Jamieson. But it had been bad enough for all of them. The heavy threat of suspension had hung over the whole school. Nobody figured Jamieson would get anything like what Forsyth would get, but there was no doubt about it: they would both be punished.

And yet not many people in the school blamed Jamieson. All of them had heard, from time to time, the sickening voice of racial prejudice; many of them had wanted to do something about it, but few had. So what Jamieson had done was what a lot of other people wished they'd had the courage to do, at other times.

As the two boys walked down the stairs together, Pete knew that it had had to happen, but that it was real bad luck for this to have come just at the climax of Northwest's first season. He knew the standings by heart now. After the fight last week, Kelvin had beaten Daniel Mac 2-1, so that now Kelvin had 12 points, Daniel Mac eight, Northwest seven, St. John's six, and Gordon Bell three. Tomorrow night St. John's played Gordon Bell, but even with a win couldn't do anything more than tie Daniel. But Northwest, in this last game, could make second place and the playoffs by beating Daniel Mac. Just one more game. One more victory. Just one.

Jamieson tapped on the principal's door.

"Come in!" The principal's secretary was behind her desk. On chairs around the wall were Benny Wong, Winston Kryschuk, Pincher Martin, Rosy Duplessis, Red Turner.

Red moved his chair so Pete and Jamieson could sit near him. "They'll call us in a minute," he said. "They're going to go over to Gordon Bell this afternoon and ask questions there. The result will be announced probably either late this afternoon, or tomorrow morning."

"I hope it's not tomorrow morning," Pete said. "This waiting is killing me."

The secretary's buzzer rang. She was a pretty, attractive girl, very businesslike as she lifted her phone and listened. Then she stood up and said, "Benny Wong, would you go in please, and Mr. Turner?"

The door closed behind the two and there was a murmur of voices.

"Who's in there?" Pete asked the secretary in a low voice.

"The principals from Daniel Mac, Kelvin and St. John's, she said. "They've been appointed by the league council as a board of inquiry."

Martin spoke up. "There's nobody in the world can say Jamieson did the wrong thing."

"They'll say I did the wrong thing, all right," Jamieson said. "They might say that Forsyth was more in the wrong than me, but they'll not excuse me."

Pete looked at Jamieson's pale face. Good thing it wasn't final exams. Jamieson had had a bad week in classes. Most of the teachers had gone easy on him, because he was a good scholar and he had a good reason to be absent-minded. But still it had been a bad week.

The door opened. Wong came out and motioned his pal and linemate, Kryschuk, inside. Then he left the office without speaking. A few minutes later Kryschuk came out and Martin went in. Finally only Pete and Jamieson were left. Then, when Rosy came out and left the office, he nodded to Pete.

Inside, Mr. Anderson introduced Pete around. The tall spare man was Mr. Fashoway from Daniel Mac. He and Pete already knew one another. Mr. Essery from Kelvin was short and stocky, a square-faced, kind-looking man. Mr. Kerr from St. John's was black-haired with the build of an athlete, a big nose, a humorous glint to his eyes. Red was sitting in a corner, looking glum.

Mr. Essery seemed to be the chairman of the

inquiry. "We just want to know what you heard during the game, if anything, which would make Jamieson act as he did, Pete," he said. "Things you heard, or your opinions . . . whatever you want to say."

Pete told about what Forsyth had called Rosy. In a calm voice, he went through the game and told what he remembered, the look on Benny Wong's face after that clash in the corner, scraps of words, Rosy's unruffled reaction. At the end, he said, "By the end of the game we were all mad. But we knew that Mr. Turner was going to make an official protest and have something done and so we managed to hold our tempers."

"Except Jamieson, of course," Mr. Fashoway said.

"He held his, too, until the game was over," Red said.

"In a way," Mr. Kerr said, "that doesn't help the boy as far as this inquiry goes. It means that the attack was premeditated, rather than the result of a natural flare-up due to a hard check."

"If the referee had listened to Mr. Turner's protests earlier it wouldn't have happened," Pete said quickly.

"The referee has been reprimanded," Mr. Essery said.

There was a silence, then Mr. Essery said, "I think that's all, Pete. Tell Jamieson to come in."

Pete went out and Jamieson looked up. His face was set and pale. "It's okay," Pete said. "They're really on your side, I think." He walked back to class. He almost felt sorry for Forsyth when they went to work on him this afternoon. Each one of those men could be kind, or could be hard, or he wouldn't be given a job as a principal. And they were being kind, here. Pete had an idea that this afternoon with Forsyth would be the time when they would be hard.

The rest of the day crawled by. Pete kept looking at the clock. Jamieson didn't come back to class. At lunchtime Red told Pete that the Northwest principal had excused Jamieson from school for the rest of the day.

But there was a practice that night, and Jamieson was there. The dressing room was quiet, unlike other practice nights. Their practice time was six o'clock. It was quarter to six when Lee Vincent tapped on the door and entered. He walked directly down to Red and showed him a typewritten sheet of paper. Red read it, then asked Lee, "Is it okay if I read it to them?"

"Sure," Lee said.

Everyone was listening, so Red didn't have to

call for attention. Jamieson had gone suddenly pale. DeGruchy was yanking savagely at a skate-lace. Fat hoisted himself up on an equipment trunk to listen.

"Lee had been over at Gordon Bell all afternoon waiting for the results of the inquiry," Red said. "They've just given it to him. It will probably be on the radio tonight, too. Here it is. . . ." He paused. "It names the people first, the three principals. . . . Then it says . . . 'The league council takes a most severe view of the incident which happened at the end of last week's first hockey game, when Jamieson of Northwest made what seemed to most onlookers an unprovoked attack on Forsyth of Gordon Bell.' "

"Unprovoked!" Fat exclaimed, and there was a murmur from the others.

Red went on. " 'However, upon investigation it was found that during the game Forsyth had repeatedly made insulting racially based references to one of the Northwest players. We feel that his actions in this regard should bring shame to himself and those of his teammates who heard him and allowed him to go on. Referees in the league have been instructed that any such further incidents are to be met by immediate ejection of the player involved from a game, and indefinite suspension from all sports. Forsyth has submitted a written apology which will be forwarded to all the players who were objects of his verbal attacks, and because of this apology has been allowed to remain a student at Gordon Bell Collegiate.' "

Red paused, looked around the quiet dressing room at more than a dozen boys ready for the practice, each intent on his words. "And here's what they did," he said. " 'Forsyth has been suspended from all sports in Gordon Bell until school reopens next autumn. This, because he is a leading member of the Gordon Bell basketball and track teams, is considered a justly heavy penalty. Jamieson, although his attack on Forsyth now can be understood as being in defence of one of his teammates, should have allowed the school board to punish Forsyth instead of taking violent punishment into his own hands. Accordingly, he has been suspended for a period of one game.' " Red was finished. He looked around the room.

DeGruchy stood up. "As captain of this team," he said, "I would like to say that although we'll miss Gord for the game tomorrow night, we all feel that he did the right thing, no matter what the school board says."

Red looked around for a few seconds longer, handed the paper back to Lee Vincent, who had been standing beside him. Lee folded the statement and put it in his pocket.

Red said, "All right, we're due on the ice."

And then he turned to Spunska, and it came so fast that Bill, intent on what had been going on, was as surprised as the others. "You're elected, Bill. You'll dress for the game tomorrow."

CHAPTER 18

The next night, when St. John's and Gordon Bell faced off for the first game of the doubleheader, the Northwest team sat in a long row high in the Northwest section. At one end of the row was Martin, then Berton, Wong, Kryschuk, Mitchell, Big Canoe, Duplessis, Jamieson, Pete, Spunska, DeGruchy, Brabant, Lawrence, Paterson, Bell and Buchanan. They were all quiet and tense, talking in low voices among themselves. Pete could feel how tense Spunska was. He was being pitchforked into the toughest position any rookie could find himself in. DeGruchy and Pete had talked it over, alone, a few minutes earlier.

"We won't say a thing to him now about what he's to remember," DeGruchy said.

Pete agreed. "Better to have him out there doing things instinctively, instead of trying to remember things we tell him."

Mr. and Mrs. Gordon and Sarah were a few rows below them. Lee Vincent, in the press box, glanced once or twice at the row of Northwesters, feeling what was in their minds now. Red and Fat were down in the dressing room.

Spunska said, "My father decided not to come. He moved the radio into mother's room. They'll be listening." He exhaled a long breath. "Gosh, I hope I do all right."

"You'll do all right," Pete said.

The game started. Pete watched McMillan of St. John's and Bush of Gordon Bell battle for the puck. Gordon Bell got the first goal, a neat passing play from Bevan to Jones. Then McMillan connected on a long shot to tie the score. Halfway through the period St. John's scored again, and in the second period, while the tension in the Northwest team grew and grew, St. John's poured in four more. The score was 6-1, the game in the bag for St. John's, when the second period ended and the Northwest players filed to the dressing room.

In the corridor they mixed with Daniel Mac players heading for their dressing room, too. Lee Vincent wandered around in the halls a few minutes, then went back to watch the third period of the St. John's game.

The Northwest dressing room was quiet. The players dressed without talking more than was necessary. Pete was among the first ready and waiting, and he had a knot in his stomach.

"Wish the game would start," he said to Bell. "Boy, have I got butterflies."

Bell just nodded. "Me, too. I've got four-engined butterflies!"

Spunska sat silently with beads of sweat standing out on his forehead.

A prolonged burst of cheering from above was followed by the sound of skates clumping downstairs. Fat went out and came back to report that the score hadn't changed. So now St. John's was tied in the standings with Daniel Mac. But they were out of it. A tie or a win for Daniel Mac would put the Daniels into the playoffs with Kelvin. A win for Northwest would put Northwest in the playoffs. *Only* a win.

For the last few minutes, Pete and DeGruchy went to sit with Spunska. Benny Wong and Rosy Duplessis came over, too. But there was nothing to say. They just sat there with the fire slowly building inside of them until Red headed for the door. He paused there, with his hand on the doorknob and spoke. "I've never had to tell you guys how to do it, all season," he said. "You've always known. And you know as well as I do what this one means."

They filed out. The Daniel Mac team already was on the ice. Pete skated through them, greeting some of the boys he knew. He spoke to Ron Maclean.

"Funny us winding up in a situation like this, eh?" Pete said.

Ron grinned ruefully. "I don't know how you

guys have done it," he said. "But tonight'll be different."

"Don't be too sure," Pete said.

They warmed up. The rink was jammed. The news of the suspension of Jamieson just before this all-important final game had been a blow to Northwest's hopes, but the news that he would be replaced by a boy nobody had seen but most sports-page readers knew about from Lee Vincent's earlier story, had given the game an extra interest. All through the stands, people were talking it up. "Wonder how this kid'll make out."

"Real tough luck on Northwest. They were really hot."

"Can't blame that Jamieson kid. I'd do the same myself."

"Daniel Mac really murdered them last month, though, 9–3."

"But that was with Pete Gordon out. He's half the team."

The referee checked the nets. The tension grew and grew. Spunska took a shot on the goal and it missed but hit the back boards with a resounding crash.

"That new kid's got a hard shot!"

"Clumsy on his skates, though."

"Looks clumsy, all right. . . . But he gets around pretty fast."

Pete was watching Spunska, through the

warm-up, with an awareness so keen that it was as if he'd never seen the boy before. He remembered all the morning workouts, weeks of them. He wished now that he'd gotten a couple of forwards to come in the mornings, too, so they could have worked Spunska and DeGruchy against complete forward lines. But it was too late to think what might have been done. Anyway, Spunska had got that kind of training in the team workouts. It would do. Pete had an instinctive feeling that if Spunska ever was to play a great hockey game, this would be it, his first. He had that kind of spirit. He had ability, and more than anyone Pete had ever known, Spunska wanted to be a good hockey player.

The whistle blew to start the game.

Pete skated to centre, exchanged a few words with Bell and Buchanan, looked back at the defence. DeGruchy and Spunska stood there together. It was daring, in a way, to put Spunska on the starting lineup. But Red had decided that way. DeGruchy was his best defenceman. If anybody could hold up a new boy, it was DeGruchy. Besides, in all those mornings at the rink DeGruchy and Spunska had worked together. They knew one another's styles of play. Sometimes an ounce of understanding is worth ten pounds of experience.

The centre opposing Pete was big Blackie White, second string last year when Pete was top centre at Daniel Mac. His wings were George Peters, another veteran, and Chum Blackburn, a new kid, a tall boy with long arms and a thin face, now talking it up with the others. Ron Maclean and Campbell McKay were on defence, Lonny Riel in goal.

He noted all this in a few seconds while the referee held the puck. Pete's stick was down in the centre circle, with White's. His eyes were on the puck in the referee's right hand. Down it came! The game was on!

White got the draw. As he wheeled and drove forward, Pete poked the puck away from him, across to Bell, but Blackburn intercepted the pass and with a quick burst of speed tore in on the Northwest defence. Pete, wheeling, stride for stride with White to guard against a pass to centre, saw DeGruchy wave his stick at Spunska to cover the puck carrier while DeGruchy stayed in centre, watching for the pass. It was a first big test for Spunska, seconds after the game started. And Pete saw Spunska with his head up and his arms wide, stepping toward Blackburn, eyes on Blackburn's, ignoring the kid's dipsy-doodling shift, and there was a solid crash and a sudden roar from the crowd as Blackburn went down.

But the puck went between Spunska's legs. He wheeled fast and was back for it, but White drove into the corner after it, too. Spunska turned quickly and shot the puck against the boards so that it came back to Pete's stick and he was away. At the Daniel Mac defence, with White slashing at the puck from the side, trying to catch him, Pete looked up to place his wings, saw Maclean coming for him, shifted and passed to Buchanan, who got the first shot on goal. It was turned away quickly to the wing by Riel. Blackburn tried to get out, but failed. Maclean recovered and dashed down centre ice, Pete chasing him.

At the defence Ron got around Spunska but ran right into DeGruchy and the thud could be heard in the press box fifty feet away.

"Two minutes gone," Lee Vincent remarked. "And already two of the toughest checks of the season."

Then Spunska was away on his first rush. There was a chuckle of laughter in the crowd at his clumsiness, as he picked up the puck and broke into the queer half-run that he always used to get up speed, but the chuckle turned to a rising cheer as Spunska tore down centre ice and into the Daniel Mac defence.

Just like that first time he got the puck, the first practice, Pete was thinking, speeding up fast behind Spunska. Except that now he knows what to do. I hope. . . .

Spunska did know what to do. As he crossed the Daniel Mac blueline he looked behind him and saw Pete and just as he hit the Daniel Mac defence he dropped back a pass and for an instant the puck sat there two feet inside the blueline. Then Spunska hit the defence and he and Maclean went down together, and Pete was on the puck, passing to Bell, who swept in around Cam McKay.

He was in the clear!

He sped in, waiting for Riel to make a move, but Riel didn't move. Bell desperately swept across in front of the goal and tried a backhand, but the goalie had outguessed him, and he was too far past. The shot was wide.

The teams started changing lines on the go. Berton replaced Pete, and then Bell kept the puck in the Daniel Mac zone and finally held it against the boards so the line change could be completed. Big Canoe and Mitchell joined Berton, and Lawrence and Duplessis went to defence.

Pete sank down beside Spunska. "You did fine, boy."

"Nice going, Bill," said Red, behind them. "Keep it up."

"That Ron Maclean can sure hit!" Spunska said.

Pete grinned, and looked across the rink to the Daniel Mac bench. "He's probably saying the same thing about you."

The cheers rolled around them in constant

thunder. Check, check, skate, shoot, save, shoot. . . . Pete's line was on again, a few minutes later, then off. Paterson made a great save on Blackburn and smothered the puck when White tried to bat in the rebound. Benny Wong was in close and fired point-blank at Riel, who saved. But this was like a playoff game. Both sides were playing it cagey, taking no chances they could help. The first period ended with no score. As the players left the ice the Northwest cheerleaders went into their act, and the Daniel Macs answered, and in the press box Lee Vincent sat and listened quietly, feeling the excitement. He smiled when he heard the new version of the Northwest song.

Oh, Northwest is not in the basement,
Not we, oh not we, oh not we!
We're new but we're bound for the playoffs,
You'll see, oh you'll see, oh you'll see!

"They had to change that song," a man beside Lee said dryly. "I don't imagine they're sorry, though."

"No."

When Pete came back to the ice in the second period his tension was gone. Funny. The whole season had been going through his mind, during the space between periods. He looked back now and thought of how sad he'd been three months ago about leaving Daniel Mac, and now he was skating his heart out to beat them. He skated to the boards and waved to his parents and Sarah. Spunska, skating slowly along the boards, looked up and waved, too, with a half-shy, half-proud smile. And Pete noticed that Sarah was still watching Spunska, when the big boy had gone by, and her lips were moving as she talked excitedly to her parents.

There'd been no penalties in the first period. In the second Ron Maclean tangled with Winston Kryschuk and fell to the ice, and while he fell he was yelling at the referee to make sure he'd seen. It was a trip all right – accidental, but a trip anyway. Kryschuk disconsolately went to the penalty box, and Daniel Mac turned on the heat.

Pete and Pincher Martin were sent out to kill off the penalty, with DeGruchy and Rosy Duplessis on defence. Pete got the draw on the face-off, but lost it to White, and White shot the puck into the Northwest zone and the Daniels piled in after it. For a minute there was bedlam. Shots rained on Paterson from all angles, but he kept them all out. Pete tried to get out with the puck. Ron Maclean knocked him down. Martin tried, but lost it to White at the blueline. DeGruchy tried to shoot it the length of the ice to relieve the pressure. Blackburn knocked it down with his hand and blasted a shot on goal.

Then there was a mad scramble around the goal and with Blackburn lying in the goal crease George Peters slipped the puck into an open corner. The goal judge's light flashed on! There was a groan from the Northwest stands, a thunderous yell from the Daniel Mac section, but the referee was in there fast, waving his arms that the goal was disallowed, just as DeGruchy and Pete descended on him to protest that Blackburn had been lying in the crease.

The Daniel Macs didn't protest. They knew Blackburn had been in the crease, although scrambling to get out. The crease, marked by a line painted in a rectangle in front of the goal, was three feet deep and seven feet across; only the goalie was allowed in it unless the puck was there.

"Lucky!" Maclean grumbled to Pete, skating by.

Pete said nothing. It had been lucky.

Fired by that luck, the shorthanded Northwesters kept the puck in centre ice or the Daniel Mac zone until Kryschuk came back from the penalty box. Now Daniel Mac was playing it cagier than ever, making sure they never got trapped in the Northwest zone.

The second period also ended without a score.

Downstairs, Red said, "You've got to get a goal this period, gents. A tie is all Daniel needs. Even a scoreless tie."

And the team came back for the third period determined that, whatever happened, it would be no tie.

But the minutes ticked away. Northwest threw the game wide open. Every time the puck went into the Daniel Mac zone all the Northwesters moved up to the blueline in a power play. One of Spunska's hard drives from the blueline bounced off two or three players and the crowd noise suddenly rose and fell as the puck skidded within inches of an open corner of the net. When the Daniels got it out they wouldn't even follow it into the Northwest zone unless there was a real chance for a break. Pete was thinking that in a way this was lucky, not making the burden too heavy on the green member of the defence, and then suddenly this green member of the defence took control of the game.

It was a play following the strict pattern of bar-the-door hockey Daniel Mac had been employing. White carried the puck into centre ice, saw no chance for a safe pass, and shot a long roller at the Northwest net. Paterson stopped it easily and looked around for someone to give it to. And everybody saw Spunska coming back full tilt towards his own net, picking up the puck, making the quick turn not gracefully, but well, and without slackening speed he was flying down the ice into the hitherto impregnable lineup the Daniels had set up in the centre zone, gathering speed, pushing the puck in front of him, not letting it get too far in front. The rest of the Northwest team rallied with him, turned, flying, and the Daniels were taken by surprise, unable to get up speed fast enough to match Spunska going in.

Just before he hit the blueline Spunska glanced up to place possible pass receivers; the Daniel Mac defence opened a little to cover the wings and Spunska saw his chance. He gave the puck a last little shove and then leaped in the air to get over the sticks of the defencemen closing in on him too late. Pete struggled to get through, too, but was turned around, and he saw Spunska lining up the shot and then blasting. Riel came out to cut down the angle of the shot and barely got his skate on the puck as Spunska drove it at the small opening. The puck bounded from Riel's skate to the sideboards, Spunska went in after it, passed out to centre, and in the next two minutes he was everywhere in the Daniel Mac zone, falling down, getting up, shouting, tearing from side to side. It was as if all the first part of the game had been a slow build-up for his confidence, and now he had it, and he was in command.

Pete thought of Spunska's parents, listening to the game; thought of all the mornings at the rink, and there was a lump in his throat.

Five minutes left in the game, still a scoreless tie. Four minutes. Spunska rushed dangerously again, was relieved, sat fretting with DeGruchy on the bench, sprang to his feet when Wong was in for a close shot, then Martin. With two minutes to go Spunska and DeGruchy went back to the ice. Pete and Bell and Buchanan replaced the Martin line. Spunska made another ferocious rush, got another shot, again was turned back by the cool Riel.

Most of the six thousand people were standing now, their voices lost in the uproar. Lee chewed his pencil. Red Turner had his hat off and was twisting it into a shapeless mess. Sarah Gordon gripped her father's arm hard. He sat quietly, watching his old school and his son's new school fight it out to the end.

Sixty-five seconds left to play. In their anxiety, the Northwesters had committed an offside on a long pass from DeGruchy to Bell across the red line. The face-off was in the Northwest zone.

Red debated if he should change his lines, for this last push. Put on somebody fresh. He sent Big Canoe out and told him to call DeGruchy to the bench.

Grouchy skated up, ready to protest if he was being taken off.

Red said, "Tell Paterson that as soon as we get the puck out of our own end he's to come to the bench. We'll replace him with a forward. A tie's no good to us."

As DeGruchy skated back to tell Paterson, the rink was suddenly quiet and Pete, standing on the blueline, trying to relax for the last all-important minute, could hear the voice of the radio broadcaster in the gondola in the rafters, an excited voice, and again he could imagine it sounding in the room at Spunska's home, Mrs. Spunska in the bed, Mr. Spunska in a chair, waiting, as everyone waited.

The referee tooted his whistle. Pete went in to take the face-off. He had to get this one. He did. He batted White's stick away and whirled with it and from the corner of his eye saw Paterson leaving his nets, cautiously, ready to get back in case his side lost the puck.

No goalie, now! All or nothing!

At centre he looked up and the whole Northwest team was with him, Bell and Buchanan and Spunska and DeGruchy, skating fast, eagerly, a step behind him.

Paterson reached the bench. Hurry Berton sprang to the ice. Pete stick-handled across the blueline, holding the puck as long as possible, waiting for everyone to get into position. Then he passed to Berton, coming in, and Berton eluded a check and shot. The puck was whacked back to the blueline to DeGruchy, who shot. Riel kicked it out. Buchanan was in for the rebound, Riel batted it off to the side. Spunska drove in, was blocked, fell, and passed to Berton. But Maclean, desperate, his red hair flying out behind him, beat Berton to the pass.

Forty seconds left.

Maclean got his stick on the puck and DeGruchy was falling back to cover a possible rush on the open goal when Spunska, kneeling on the ice, halfway to his feet, dove full length on the ice and hooked the puck away from Maclean again and sent it over to Pete. Pete took a quick glance at the goal. No holes. He feinted a shot and laid the puck back to Spunska, who was on his feet now, and Spunska got set for a drive and in that instant, waiting for the shot, everybody froze.

Spunska leaned for the shot, but didn't shoot!

His quick slap pass went across the goalmouth to Berton, who was almost in the clear. Berton took the puck and shifted, all in one motion, to get away from his check, fired a quick backhand. The rebound came out to Pete. His ears were full of the screaming excitement of the crowd. He shot, panting, anxious. The rebound came out to DeGruchy. He fired.

Spunska shot. Riel dove to try to grab the puck and end this furious rally and in the instant before he got his hand on it, Spunska flicked it away from the groping fingers and Pete twisted free from Ron Maclean. He got it. He looked up. Riel was sprawled on the ice, the goal wide open. As Pete was hit, he shot over Riel. The puck hit the back of the net. The red light for the goal went on a second before the blue light and buzzer to end the game.

The loudspeaker blared out above the noise, with the slow British voice of Arthur Mutchison.

"Goal for Northwest! Scored by Gordon, assist from Spunska. Final score: Northwest 1, Daniel Mac no score. Northwest wins the second place in the playoffs."

The crowd drowned out the last of it. Camera lights flashed. Red Turner dazedly tried to straighten out his hat, wondering how on earth it had got into this mess. Fat sat alone on the bench. He hadn't followed the others when they poured onto the ice. He wasn't sure he had enough strength left to walk. He clutched the bundle of spare hockey sticks, wondering if ever again in his life he'd feel like this.

Spunska burst through the crowd and put his arm around Pete's shoulders and hugged him. DeGruchy came up between them, separated them, and hugged them both.

He was laughing, almost deliriously happy.

"Only one thing wrong, Pete!" he yelled above the crowd. "You must be disappointed that your good old Daniel Mac didn't make the playoffs!"

"Sure!" Pete said, grinning. "Sure, sure. . . ." Daniel Mac was a long way behind him now.

CHAPTER 19

Saturday morning was bleak with snow and cold, but it was only ten o'clock when Spunska arrived at Pete's home.

"Hi, champ," Pete said.

Spunska grinned, embarrassed.

DeGruchy came next, then Bell and Buchanan. Then Rosy Duplessis arrived in his father's car with Benny Wong and Winston Kryschuk and Adam Lawrence and Gordon Jamieson. "Just going by," Rosy said. "Of course it is just by chance I have with me these other characters."

Paterson, Brabant, Martin, Fat, Berton, Big Canoe, Mitchell – they all came. They sat on the floor, in the chairs, against the wall. Pete's dad came in and looked around and then went into the kitchen.

"Talk about a barrel full of monkeys," he said, smiling, to his wife. "They never made a noise like that bunch."

At eleven-thirty Lee Vincent arrived.

At the door, he said, "Hi, Pete. I brought

around a bunch of those pictures our photographer took in the dressing room last night. I'm delivering them. Came here first. One each, with our compliments."

"Come on in," Pete said. "They're all here."

Inside, Lee looked around the room and laughed aloud. "A meeting," he said. "Figuring out how you'll beat Kelvin in the playoff?"

"Is the date set yet?" Grouchy asked.

"Not yet."

"We won't worry about that, anyway," Grouchy said. "We're in. That's all that counts right now."

For some reason, then, everyone looked at Spunska. He flushed, then said, "My mother is up today. The first time in two months. The doctor said I should have got into the game before, it was better than his medicine!"

They all laughed. Lee handed around the pictures. Then he said he had to go, it was time to eat.

Pete tried to get some of the others to stay, but they couldn't. When they were gone, he looked at the picture. He'd seen pictures like it before, different faces, but the same picture, a picture of boys who had won what they wanted to win.

Sarah came in, and looked over his shoulder for a minute.

"There's your guy," he said, pointing to Spunska.

She blushed. "I know where there are some thumbtacks," she said.

They went upstairs together to Pete's room, with the picture and the thumbtacks, and looked at the crowded walls of Pete's room.

"Mr. Vincent said the school has ordered one, too," Sarah said. "They're having it framed. It'll be the first picture to go up in the halls at Northwest."

Pete grinned. It was one more thing to be happy about. He selected a place near the head of his bed and tacked the picture of Northwest's first hockey team to his bedroom wall.

Exciting Books from M&S Paperbacks

SCRUBS ON SKATES by Scott Young
High school hockey star Pete Gordon finds himself on the worst team in the league when the board of education changes the school boundaries. Slowly, however, Pete and his Northwest High "scrubs" turn themselves into potential champions...
0-7710-9088-9 • $5.99

BOY ON DEFENCE by Scott Young
The exciting sequel to *Scrubs on Skates*. When highly regarded newcomer Cliff Armstrong joins the Northwest High hockey team, everyone thinks Northwest is a shoo-in to win the city championship. But tempers are tested when Cliff feuds with teammates Pete Gordon and Bill Spunska...
0-7710-9089-7 • $5.99

A BOY AT THE LEAF'S CAMP by Scott Young
High schooler Bill Spunska gets the shock – and the opportunity – of his life when the Toronto Maple Leafs invite him to their training camp in Peterborough, Ont. The bestselling companion to *Boy on Defence* and *Scrubs on Skates*.
0-7710-9090-0 • $5.99

FROZEN FIRE by James Houston
Young Matthew Morgan and his Inuit "brother," Kayak, face almost certain death in the forbidding Arctic as they search for Matthew's missing father, a geologist.
0-7710-4244-2 • $5.99

BLACK DIAMONDS by James Houston
Matt Morgan and Kayak join Matt's father and Charlie, the helicopter pilot, in a quest to find gold on Baffin Island. However, when the boys strike oil instead, a disaster threatens to cost all of them their lives. The sequel to *Frozen Fire*.
0-7710-4248-5 • $5.99

Exciting Books from M&S Paperbacks

ICE SWORDS by James Houston
Matt and Kayak spend an exciting Arctic summer scubadiving under the sea ice and helping an American scientist study migrating whales. A huge shark, however, threatens to bring their summer to a disastrous end. Companion volume to *Frozen Fire* and *Black Diamonds*.
0-7710-4254-X • $5.99

OWLS IN THE FAMILY by Farley Mowat
A young boy's pet menagerie grows out of control with the addition of two lovable but feisty pet owls named Weeps and Wol.
0-7710-6693-7 • $5.99

THE DOG WHO WOULDN'T BE by Farley Mowat
"At some early moment of his existence Mutt concluded there was no future in being a dog." With that, Mutt and his "master," a young Farley Mowat, take the reader on a series of hilarious and hair-raising adventures.
0-7710-6665-1 • $6.99

THE BOAT WHO WOULDN'T FLOAT
by Farley Mowat
It seemed like a good idea at the time. Tired of a landlubber's life, Farley Mowat would find a boat in Newfoundland and sail it to Lake Ontario. What Farley found was the worst boat in the world, and its inadequacies threatened to drive him mad . . .
0-7710-6661-9 • $7.99

NEVER CRY WOLF by Farley Mowat
Flown in alone to study the wolves of the Canadian subarctic, young Farley Mowat arrives heavily armed expecting to find roaming packs of vicious carnivores. To Farley's – and the reader's – delight, however, the wolves seem reluctant to live up to their reputation . . .
0-7710-6663-5 • $6.99